THE HIT

THE HIT

a novel by **JULIAN MAYFIELD**

The Vanguard Press, New York

This book is for

my father and mother

Hudson and Annie Mayfield

Magically greased, out of the locks
and chains of definitions, slips the
personal I. In my Harlem, therefore,
find the Race, the Group, but, more,
find Me.

I, too, chase my dream, wrestle with it,
give it shape, but seldom taste it.

Not invisible then, nor yet outside,
but, like yourselves, searching in this
hell of earth, consumed with doing,
enmeshed by my personal Me,
terribly afraid, painfully alone.

THE HIT

1

Hubert Cooley was the superintendent of four tenement buildings on One hundred and twenty-sixth Street in Harlem. In one of these, on the ground floor, he and his family occupied a small apartment rent free. One Saturday night during the summer, when it was very warm, he was sitting with his wife Gertrude in their living room. She had been reading the *Baptist News* for more than an hour and was not aware that her husband was staring at her. He was thinking: What a mess! How I ever came to marry this woman I will never know. Imagine living with her for twenty-five years! How did I ever stand it?

"I think I'll walk a little," he announced suddenly.

"All right," said Gertrude.

Leaving the apartment, Hubert told himself that Gertrude was not—and never had been—the woman for him. She had not even looked up from her paper when he spoke. She had not said Good night, God bless you, or Good night, Dog. He certainly had no reason to feel guilty about going to call on another woman.

Out on the street Hubert thought: Nothing short of death can keep a Negro in his house on a Saturday night. By this he did not mean himself, but his neighbors who were lounging on the front stoops and in the open windows of their apartments. They were laughing and talking too loud, and some of them were drinking beer and wine. They greeted him, but he only nodded his head and walked on. They were not his friends, but Gertrude's. No, indeed! He minded his own business and he hoped they would mind theirs. He had no use for the trifling kind of Negro; they did not know how to act in public. Even now, as late as it was, their dirty little kids were playing in the streets, catching ball, pitching pennies, and playing three-card molly under the lamplight. As he crossed Lenox Avenue a very black boy driving an Oldsmobile tried to run him down. This was convincing proof that young Negroes went crazy as soon as they got behind the wheel of a car.

Sister Clarisse lived alone in a small two-room apartment near Seventh Avenue. Her husband had been a deacon at Little Calvary Baptist Church before he passed on to glory. Both Sister Clarisse and Hubert's wife Gertrude were very active in the affairs of Little Calvary. They were members of both The Willing Workers' Society and The Ladies' Auxiliary. Sometimes on Sundays they were referred to from the pulpit as "pillars" of the church, but to Hubert they were as different as night and day. Sister Clarisse was the kind of woman he should have married: sweet, gentle, and, most important, very feminine. She did not give a man a hard way to go, by contradicting him, arguing with him all the time. Gertrude was a thorn in a man's side, bothersome, constantly after him to do this or that. Hubert firmly believed that a man ought to have peace from his old lady and not a lot of lip.

Sister Clarisse's apartment was a first-floor front just above the sidewalk. This evening she was sitting in the window seat fanning herself. She laughed and said, "Why, Mister Hubert! What in the world are you doing over here?"

He answered that he just happened to be walking by, and she wanted to know why he did not come in and sit a while. He could see nothing wrong with this idea and soon he was seated beside her.

Sister Clarisse had lived alone for several years, and she enjoyed casual flirtations. It certainly was not her fault if some of the brothers happened to pass her apartment now and then. Keeping them at a respectable distance, she possessed a definite charm they could not and did not want to resist. A pleasant-looking, light-brown woman in her forties, she had a dark mole on one cheek that they never failed to notice. Hubert was fond of her high musical laugh. If he made a joke, she would spread her hands and laugh in a Southern way, saying, "You stop it now, Brother Hubert, coming over here and making a girl laugh herself almost to death over your foolishness." He would go to almost any lengths to make her laugh, because sometimes when she was really tickled she would slap him on his knee, and that would make him feel warm all over.

After saying good night to her, Hubert decided to walk down Lenox Avenue; he never wanted to go directly home after leaving Sister Clarisse. At the corner of One hundred and twenty-fifth Street he stopped to listen to a Black Nationalist who stood on a small platform making a speech to an audience of thirty or forty people. The Nationalist was a fine-looking man with glistening black skin.

His mustache was thick like his eyebrows and trimmed neat and sharp. His tongue seemed crimson against the ebony of his skin. In a broad West Indian accent his screaming words slashed at his listeners: "Black mawn, wake up! Wake up! Drive this gowddawm white mawn out of Harlem where he comes and takes your mawney, mawn, out of your pockets. He molests your women while little children got no decent schools and go without food in their belly. Wake up! You hear me? I say, black mawn, black womawn! Wake up and recognize Africa as your true home. Do you hear me? Wake up!"

When the Nationalist finished, Hubert was so moved that he could not help joining in the loud applause, although he did not want to go to Africa or any other place where there were so many Negroes. He walked on.

At One hundred and twenty-fourth Street an old man with a clean-shaven head had somehow pushed taps into his bare feet and was dancing on the sidewalk. He must once have been a professional, for he moved effortlessly and gracefully in his small circle, setting up a machine-gun rhythm with heel and toe. Now he mumbled, "Pick up on this. Hey! . . . one . . . one . . . one two . . . one one one two two." Sometimes he would whirl six or seven times, tapping as he went. As he settled down he would shake his head sadly and say:

> *"Old Bill Robinson is dead and gone*
> *But Lightfoot Charlie dances on."*

Then he would compliment himself with a raspy laugh and a loud slap on his leg: "Goddog your time, boy. You know one thing? You're a dancing fool." He wore a white shirt with broad green stripes and pink trousers rolled up to his knees so everyone could see that the sounds were coming from his bare feet. But no one paid him any attention, and the old hat he had placed on the sidewalk remained empty. Hubert felt instant dislike for the passers-by who hardly glanced at the clownish dancer. Sure, he was foolish, but at least he was trying. Hubert felt a sudden kinship for the man. He dropped a dime in the hat.

Farther down Lenox Avenue a young woman brushed against him with her hips. "Hi, Pops." Hubert did not know her and resented the familiarity. And who was she calling Pops? He ignored her and walked on. At One hundred and twentieth Street he stopped to listen to singing that poured out of a little store-front church with white painted windows. As the congregation inside shouted the words, they stamped their feet and clapped their hands.

> *Lordy, Lordy, they keep crucifying you.*
> *Lordy, Lordy, they do it every day.*
> *Atom Bombs and H-bombs,*
> *Crucifying You, Lord, in every way.*

A crayoned sign on the door said that this was the Happiness Holiness Church. Inside, the song went on and on. Women screamed and fainted. Everybody shouted and the song went on.

At One hundred and fourteenth Street in a tenement hallway a dark-brown boy was kissing a copper-colored girl. It was a long, sensuous kiss, and both of them moved their bodies in time with mambo music from a nearby jukebox. Hubert strongly disapproved of this kind of carrying on. No wonder, he thought, our young people find it so hard to get along. They don't know how to act.

Farther on, Hubert saw a barroom where the Negroes seemed to be standing three deep. The jukebox, as usual, was turned up full volume, and they were laughing and shouting over its noise. Such scenes always disgusted Hubert. All these years of freedom had not taught them the most important thing about being free: to hold on to your money and make it work for you. Wasn't that the way the big white man stayed on top? Did you ever catch him spending a dime unless he expected to make two more? If the good Lord would let Hubert catch one of those lucky numbers he would show everybody that there was one Negro who knew how to put his money to work.

As Hubert neared the park he began to hear Spanish from groups of people clustered on the sidewalk. He wondered why foreign people would choose to settle in Harlem. Many of them seemed light-complexioned enough to live anywhere they wished. If Hubert had been blessed with fairer skin he would have crossed the color line and never returned.

It was a soft night, a gentle night on Central Park West. Girls and boys strolled arm in arm. Hubert sat down next to a man and a woman on one of the long benches. His thoughts turned to San Francisco, where he was going if he ever won at the numbers. Once someone had told him that Negroes had very good opportunities in the West. Some of them had their own businesses and all of them were industrious because that was the kind of city 'Frisco was—a place where willingness to work was rewarded. The very thought of himself on the West Coast made him feel good. Impulsively he turned to the woman sitting beside him.

"You ever been to San Francisco?"

The woman was startled. She turned to her companion, a man of about thirty, who leaned forward so he could get a better look at Hubert.

"What did you say, fella?"

Hubert didn't answer. He couldn't understand why the man sounded so belligerent.

"Do you know this lady?"

"No, I don't," Hubert replied. Then he realized that the man thought Hubert was flirting with the young woman. That was silly. After all, a man his age . . .

"Then what the hell are you talking to her for?"

The man stood up. He had a wide, tan face and a lower lip that jutted out.

The woman said, "Aw, I don't think he meant nothing, J.C."

"I think you'd better beat it, buddy."

"Aw, J.C. . . ." She looked pityingly at Hubert.

"Gowan, Pop," said J.C. "Beat it."

What was there to do? Hubert got up and walked away. It was just like a Negro of that low type to show off in front of his girl. Hubert wished he were younger and nearly the same size as that big yellow bastard. He would have beaten J.C. until his socks dropped off.

Behind him Hubert heard, "Aw, baby, the poor little guy didn't mean nothing. Just a little off, that's all."

"This park is full of nothing but freaks," said J.C. "This whole city is full of all kinds of freaks. They ought to exterminate 'em all."

Hubert walked down Central Park West. The farther he walked, the less he felt inclined to return to Harlem. And so it happened that he never went back home that Saturday night.

2

Hubert Cooley had but one obsession, and that was to leave family, home, and Harlem as far behind as possible and create a new life for himself. He had lived with this idea for more than five years. He wanted to go to another city, San Francisco preferably, and set himself up in some small business. For this he had some qualifications. During the nineteen thirties, he had, at various times,

owned two grocery stores, a dry-cleaning shop, and
a poolroom. The fact that they had all failed did
not disturb him. He believed that he only needed
a few thousand dollars and some luck. So, whenever he could, he would bet as much as five or
six dollars a day on the numbers. Since he hardly
earned this much from his job, it is understand-
able that people thought him peculiar.

His luck was about to change. It was all in the
hands of God, with whom Hubert had a rather odd
relationship, one that would have shocked the
members of Little Calvary had they known about
it. Devoutly believing that God was responsible
for everything that happened on earth, Hubert
therefore concluded it was God who had done him
wrong. This, although He knew that Hubert deserved better breaks, for surely industrious, honest Hubert was more worthy than those Negroes
who had climbed up the financial ladder by de-
vious means. Hubert's continuing faith depended
on God's doing something it is not recorded He
had ever done before: admit His errors and correct them. Once this was done, Hubert would
surely have a change of luck.

So Hubert never fell on his knees to pray. His
Sunday attendance at Little Calvary was more
from habit than anything else. When Hubert heard
the congregation sending up fervent prayers,
he felt they were all strangers shouting at a personal friend of his. He himself talked with God

any time it came to mind: standing in a crowd, working, walking down the street—anywhere. True, their long-standing relationship was undergoing considerable strain. Hubert had not received his due reward. Soon it would be too late; already he was more than fifty years old. But he was optimistic. Where was the meaning of life if God did not correct His errors? If Justice and Right did not triumph?

More than twenty-four hours after Hubert left home he found himself sitting on Central Park South. It was near midnight and he was tired. He sat on a bench and crossed his legs. He had been to Brooklyn, Queens, and the Bronx, and now he was thinking about returning home. He had never spent the night away from home before, and Gertrude was bound to be worried. But this did not bother him. It was simply that his money was gone and he would soon be hungry again.

On Central Park South the skyscraper hotels look northward over the park toward Harlem and the Bronx. These hotels are like high glass fortresses that guard Manhattan's sparkling midtown district. What fascinated Hubert were the penthouses. Their tiny lights peeked out into the night like small, excited eyes. He wondered what it was like to live so far above the ground. This was an exceptionally hot night, but there were probably cooling, gentle breezes up there. Certainly it was quiet—not at all like One hundred and twenty-sixth Street, where the children whooped and yelled until all hours and the Lenox Avenue drunks raised holy hallelujah every night.

Hubert had never been inside such a fine hotel as the one across the street, and only in the movies and in magazines had he seen the interiors of penthouses. But as he stared up at their lights he could easily imagine the tall, casual men and the luxurious women with their soft, clear skin. He saw them lighting cigarettes and sipping chilled drinks from thin-stemmed glasses. He heard their pleasant, educated talk and quiet, refined laughter.

Across the street a taxicab drew up before the hotel and stopped under its white light. A smiling doorman in a blue-and-white uniform helped the passengers to the sidewalk, and the taxi moved away. The guests were in their fifties. The man was short, rotund, and a little lame, it seemed, for he walked with the aid of a cane. The woman appeared taller in her dark evening dress. There was something in her hair that sparkled; for a moment the hotel lights seemed to set it afire. There was a joke between them, and they were laughing. The doorman touched his finger to his cap as they passed, but they took no notice of him. The glass doors closed behind them and they vanished into the lobby.

Hubert was excited and breathless. It had seemed such a simple thing, and yet how grand, how magnificent the whole thing was! The way the guests had stepped from the taxi and had hardly looked at the uniform that saluted and held the door for them! And they seemed so at home in that wonderful setting.

Hubert thought: If I had been born white this would have been the kind of life I would have led. He knew, of course, that there were many white people who were almost as bad off as colored folk. But Hubert could not imagine himself being both white and poor. The two things simply did not go together. Even God, who had often disappointed Hubert, could not have been so cruel and thoughtless as to bless him with fair skin and leave out the silver spoon.

It was past one o'clock in the morning when a policeman stopped to chat with the doorman of the hotel. The doorman nodded toward Hubert, and the policeman started across the street. When Hubert saw the policeman coming toward him he told himself that he had no reason to be afraid. Central Park was for the public. He was not a bum, because he had an address and he worked for a living. Nor did he look like a bum. His necktie matched his blue suit, and, as always, his shoes shone brilliantly. No one, Hubert assured himself, could mistake him for anything but what he was: a respectable citizen. Still, he could not shake off a dark guilt feeling as the uniform of the law approached.

The policeman stopped a few feet away and took a good look at the little Negro man. He saw a small dark man with tense, nervous features. He did not know exactly what to think of Hubert. Manhattan was in the middle of a heat wave, and yet this man was wearing a heavy blue pin-stripe suit. It was just possible that Hubert was one of those foreign Negroes from Haiti or Africa or someplace like that. Perhaps one of those attached to the United Nations. They caused trouble when they were mistaken for local Negroes. The policeman, a man with fifteen years' experience, decided to proceed with caution.

"Hello," he said.

"Hello," Hubert responded brusquely.

"What are you doing there?"

"I'm sitting," Hubert's voice shot back. "What did you think I was doing?" The words sounded just the way he had wanted them to, bold and self-possessed. He was pleased with himself.

"I'm just asking you a question, Pop."

"Well, I just answered you," said Hubert. "And my name ain't Pop."

"What is your name?"

"Never you mind about that."

"You're up kind of late," said the policeman.

"So are you," Hubert replied. "So what?"

Thus far Hubert felt he had done well, but a deep-seated fear of and respect for white authority made him think he might have gone just a little too far. So he added, in a protesting tone, "I ain't done nothing. I'm just sitting here where I've got a right to be."

The cop moved two or three steps closer. He was a man with blunt features. He stood easily with his hands on his belt. He was not threatening Hubert, but the little man felt intimidated anyway.

"Come on, Pop," said the policeman, "let's move it along and call it a night, what d'ya say?"

If Hubert had stood up then and walked away, the matter would have ended there and most of his dignity would have been left intact. But again the policeman had called him out of his name, and this was something he especially disliked. Besides, he reflected angrily, this *was* a public park and he *did* have a right to sit there. He *was* a citizen.

So by way of replying Hubert used an old Southern expression: "You and Lets move it along if you want to. I'm gonna stay right here." He folded his arms on his chest and recrossed his legs. You couldn't let these people push you around all your life. Sometimes you had to stand up for your rights.

Before Hubert knew what was happening, the policeman had reached down, caught him by the shoulders of his jacket, and jerked him off the bench. In one deft movement Hubert was spun around so that he was facing away from the policeman. At the same time the policeman reached under the back of Hubert's jacket and caught a grip on the trousers' belt. With this grip the policeman jerked upward, forcing the breath from Hubert and causing him to stand on tiptoe to avoid being cut between his legs by the crotch of his trousers. All this happened very quickly.

The cop's patient voice now became a growl. "A nice quiet night and then *you* had to come along."

Keeping his grip on the belt and holding it so high that Hubert was forced to walk on the very tips of his toes, the policeman began taking long steps toward Columbus Circle. Naturally Hubert knew better than to struggle against a policeman. As he was being pushed and carried along, he tried to make it appear as if he were moving under his own power, but without much success. Hubert and the policeman passed a boy strolling arm-in-arm with a blond girl. Hubert could hardly see their faces in the dark but he was certain they smiled. He could easily imagine how ridiculous he must look with his trousers pulled high above the tops of his socks. It was very undignified.

At Columbus Circle they had to pause to let the cars go by. Both of them were breathing hard. "What's your name, boy?" the cop demanded.

Then Hubert had an idea which seemed exceptionally good. Here was his way to repay the cop. He would not reveal his name.

"Just call me Pop," said Hubert.

Instead, the policeman called him a so-and-so sonofabitch and pushed the little Negro toward the precinct. But Hubert smiled fiercely. Now that he saw the cop was boiling mad, he somehow felt repaid for the indignity he was suffering. He was not afraid any more. They could pour hot oil over his naked body, set fire to his hair, and extract his teeth one by one. But he would never, never tell them his name. Never.

At the precinct station nobody seemed to care. After he refused to answer the first time, they shrugged their shoulders and continued their discussion of baseball. All of them agreed the Giants had a good team that year. One of them expressed the opinion that although the Dodgers had got off to a slow start, the team had now begun to catch fire and was steadily rolling toward the pennant. There was loud disagreement. They thoroughly reviewed the two previous seasons in defense of both points of view. This done, the desk sergeant took a look at Hubert and decided that the little man was a mental case, and all of his subordinates agreed.

"Hey, Al," the sergeant said to one of his men, "take this guy upstairs someplace."

"Okay. I'll put him with the Preacher. He's on his way to Bellevue tomorrow morning, too."

"My God, is Preacher back? What's the matter

with those guys down on Psycho? Why do they keep letting him out?"

"They say he's just an average nut and they don't have any room for average nuts. The city's full of them."

The man took Hubert by the arm and walked him up two flights of stairs. He unlocked the door of a room that smelled of disinfectant and urine. He asked Hubert if he wanted to go to the toilet, and when Hubert said no, the policeman locked Hubert inside the little room and went away.

For several minutes Hubert stood just inside the doorway without moving. Out of the darkness came broken, unintelligible murmurings that might have been used in a prayer. Suddenly the words would halt and there would be the heavy breathing of a sleeping man. In a moment the murmurings would begin again.

"Lord, the cross is heavy . . . Lord . . . Thy will be done . . . down with the devil . . . pure and white for Thee I'll keep my soul, O Lord. . . . Though he tempt me I will never . . . Most High . . . never, never . . . Amen."

The man's voice was raspy and hoarse. Could he be dangerous? Hubert turned and felt for a door knob but there was none, nor was there a place where one had been. Silently he pushed against the door, but it refused to move. He would have cried out but he was intimidated by the great stillness of the precinct building. When his eyes grew used to the darkness he saw the figure of a man on a cot with his knees drawn up in front of him. He lay facing the wall. He was praying and scratching himself. This was the Preacher.

Hubert walked quietly to the cot and let his weight down upon it slowly. He certainly had no intention of waking his roommate.

"Thy will, not mine . . . suffer . . . suffer . . . with clean hands . . . O Lord."

Hubert had never in his life been inside a prison and he had no idea what he should do next. He sat for a long time thinking about nothing in particular. He gradually became aware that he was very tired. Had he slept at all the night before? He couldn't remember. He wanted to lie back on the cot, but what if this Preacher fellow were to wake up and find Hubert off his guard? No, it would be better to stay awake. He would lie back and close his eyes for just a few seconds. He lay back, yawned, and, very much against his will, went to sleep.

This was the best dream Hubert had ever had. The others were usually so vague—confused images and sounds, like snatches from a hundred different motion pictures.

But in this dream everything was sharp and clear. Hubert and Sister Clarisse were having supper in the diner of a streamliner speeding toward San Francisco. The black waiters were smiling and bowing as they set the meal before the couple, both of whom were dressed fit to kill. She would say to him:

"Where did you get the money?"

And he would answer: "I turned the number around and played 417."

"Where did you get the money?"

"I turned the number around and played 417."

Over and over they said the same thing.

"Where did you get the money?"

"I turned the number around and played 417."

Sister Clarisse laughed and put her hand on his knee, which made him feel so good he wanted to scream. Then the train plunged into a tunnel, and Hubert and Sister Clarisse were enveloped in darkness.

He sat straight up when he remembered where he was. His fear rushed back. He had not intended to sleep. Why, anything could have happened to him as he lay there with his eyes closed. The Preacher seemed not to have moved. The man was probably not dangerous at all but some unfortunate fellow who also was being taken advantage of by the police. An automobile passed in the street below but barely disturbed the silence. The precinct building was a great sleeping thing, and Hubert lay awake in its bosom.

"Not my will . . . O Lord . . . but Thine," mumbled the Preacher.

It was true that now and then Hubert had imagined himself and Sister Clarisse together in San Francisco, but he had always put such thoughts down as wishful thinking. After all, she was a respected member of the church, a devout Christian woman. But now that the dream had again brought the idea to mind, there could certainly be no harm in thinking about it. The dream alone was evidence that he had reason to hope.

A man was a fool not to pay attention to his dreams, especially if they had numbers in them. Of course, with everybody dreaming different numbers, you could not expect them all to win. You had to be lucky and you had to have dreams so clear that there could be no doubt about what number was indicated.

Hubert lay back on the cot and cupped his head in his hands. It was true that he had played those three digits in every possible combination except in the order four, one, seven. The week before he had come close but had not hit it.

"Four-seventeen," said Hubert.

It had a good sound to it, and he felt good when he said it. If I get out of this jail in the morning, he thought, I'll start betting on 417. It probably won't pay off, but it's better to play and lose a few dollars than have it come out when you don't have a penny on it. The very day you turn chicken-hearted and decide not to play, that's the day your number always comes.

He yawned deeply and felt drowsy again. He thought of Sister Clarisse and how different his life would have been if he had married her. Well, what was it they said? Life begins at forty. Or was it fifty? Who could say? Hubert Cooley might make his big splash yet.

Tomorrow I will play 417, Hubert said to himself. My luck is overdue.

"Amen," grunted the Preacher.

3

Later the same morning, at about six o'clock, a young Negro stood before the desk sergeant of the One-hundred-and-thirty-fifth-Street police precinct station. The Negro's extremely dark features were so calm and expressionless that they seemed almost sullen. His tongue played with his bottom lip and he frequently shifted his weight from one leg to the other. The desk sergeant was a white man in his forties, a hulk of a man with boyish red cheeks set on each side of a florid face. This sergeant was not just fat, he was gigantic. The younger man was preoccupied with his personal problems, but still he could not help wondering how much fat the policeman carried about with him. Two hundred and fifty pounds? No, it was surely closer to three hundred. But weren't there weight limitations on the New York police force? When the sergeant first joined he must have been much smaller. Jesus! thought the younger man, he must have a hell of a time trying to screw a woman. He tried to imagine how the whole act would look and sound but he couldn't.

The sergeant inhaled noisily and began a long, groaning yawn as he mumbled into the telephone. The skin of his face and neck crumbled into a thousand tiny particles. He was not tired, but he wanted his morning nap. Why, he wondered, was the graveyard shift in a Harlem precinct always like the Fourth of July? They were always kicking up a fuss, these people, for the sole purpose of disturbing his five-o'clock snooze or preventing it altogether. He grumbled a bored thanks into the mouthpiece and hung up the phone. As he yawned again, more deeply this time, he let his eyes rest on the young man in front of him.

James Lee Cooley was blacker than the average American Negro. His was a liquid, whole blackness. He was a little over average height and gave the impression of being a dark reservoir of strength. His eyes were like those of a young boy: large, intelligent, uncompromising. But his manner was older, his expression almost grave. He had a singular appearance that often caused people to stare—they never knew quite what to make of him. Just now the sergeant, finishing his yawn with a soft wheeze of relief and satisfaction, was thinking: Black as pitch . . . funny-looking face . . . like sculpture . . . never know what he's thinking. Now what was it I was just talking about on the telephone? Oh, yes.

"I was right. Precinct downtown called in a few hours ago that they had picked up a fellow who fitted the description of the missing Hubert Cooley." The sergeant explained that the fellow downtown was probably a psycho, at least they thought so because he refused to give his name. What did the young man think? Could that be Hubert Cooley?

James Lee felt vaguely uncomfortable, a little disloyal. The man downtown was probably his father, and this fat sergeant was a stranger and a white man to boot. But what did it matter? Fact was fact. "Yes," he said, "that could be him."

"You could save time by going down and having a look," said the sergeant. "Of course, it's hard to tell. The city's full of crackpots. But they say this fellow fits the description. A skinny little dark-colored fellow. Been missing since Saturday night, huh? That ain't so long."

"My mother was worried about him," said James Lee. "He never stayed away before."

"Do you know how to get to the precinct on West Fifty-fourth Street right off Eighth Avenue?" asked the sergeant.

James Lee knew how to find the precinct station. Except for a very rude and unforgettable interruption of twenty-three months spent in Uncle Sam's army, he had lived in New York all of his twenty-six years. Going back and forth to school, he and his gang had raised hell on the subway trains, been chased by furious conductors through the rumbling cars. And there was that time when he had been unceremoniously kicked—literally kicked—out of the Fourteenth-Street station by two subway cops, a white one and a black one who wasted no love on schoolboys. He had hugged girls on the trains and pinched at their nipples when he thought no one was looking, girls with quick answers and chewing gum and bobby socks. And later he had ridden the trains with girls in high heels, nervous, long-legged girls, to basement parties in Brooklyn and the Bronx, to the Palace Theater and the Capitol Theater, and to the Roxy, and to frenzied Saturday nights at the Palladium. And some nights, cold, flat, gray nights, he had ridden from the Brooklyn end of the line to the

Bronx end. This was because he had been drunk and had slept past his stop. So now he said to the sergeant that he knew how to get to the precinct station downtown.

But the sergeant told him anyway, giving him detailed directions. James Lee mumbled a thank you and wondered if white people ever listened to anything Negroes said.

The sergeant punctuated his thought with: "And don't forget to get on the front of the train, d'ya hear, young fella?"

The young man reminded himself that the sergeant had been helpful, not nasty as a cop could be. So he called back a final thanks before leaving the station.

I'm all mixed up, James Lee Cooley was thinking. I don't know whether I'm coming or going. Running around, jumping into bed with everyone I can find. Hell, is that all I'm living for? I'm twenty-six years old and I don't know what it's all about yet. Damn!

As the train lurched out of the One-hundred-and-twenty-fifth-Street station he found himself a standing place in the front car near the engineer's booth. From here he could look ahead into the black tunnel. As the train was throttled forward, the tracks reflected the light of the onrushing cars and seemed to leap under their wheels. Staring straight ahead into the darkness, he imagined that

the tunnel was like his future and that he was rumbling through it headlong. He had no control over
where he was going.

There was not a single area of his life that was
going as it should. First, there were his parents.
Sure, you had to give up something for them, to
sacrifice a little, but there were limits. Hubert and
Gertrude Cooley had already lived the better part
of their lives, while the best part of his was before
him. It was not fair of his father to go wandering
away from home, nor was it fair that James Lee
should have to spend his time looking for him. Oh,
certainly, they were getting along in years and had
had some tough breaks. But how could their quiet
little lives compare with his? Two years before, he
had been in Korea in the middle of a hot shooting
war and he had damn near got himself killed. But
Hubert Cooley had never been near a war, so
what reason did he have for cracking up? James
Lee felt he had the remedy for what was ailing
his father: a good, swift kick aimed at a well-
chosen spot.

His biggest problem, he knew, had to do with
his girl Essie. He felt that if he could really make
up his mind what to do about her, everything else
would fall into place. She was waiting for him now
over in their room on One hundred and twenty-
fourth Street. She was probably still asleep, curled
snugly in their big iron bed with her knees drawn
up in front of her in that very special way she had.

But no! She was probably as mad as she could be because he had left her alone all night. By now she had called him everything but a child of God and was ready to throw things as soon as he opened the door.

Now he turned his anger on himself. A sensible guy with a girl in White Plains would keep himself free on the nights she was able to get into town. You did not have to be in love with her—he was never certain how he felt about Essie—but if you saw she was a good girl, in your corner, as the saying went, you did not go out of your way to give her a hard time. Now Essie would be hell to get along with for two or three days. In the end, of course, she would thaw, come around as she always did. He would kiss and pet her, maybe buy her a present, and she would become her usual self again. But this time winning her over would be especially difficult, and he knew he had only himself to blame.

The express train flashed through the Eighty-sixth-Street local station. James Lee became aware of a deep-seated itching in his right buttock. He squeezed closer to the engineer's booth, where he put his hand under his jacket and into his back pocket so that he could scratch himself without attracting too much attention. On hot days when he perspired he itched around the scar tissue of his wound. When this happened he would think up special curses for the army surgeons who had assured him that they had removed all the metal pieces.

Why was it that whenever he found himself alone in a room with Essie he began to feel restless, hemmed in? Sometimes he told himself that he loved Essie and that he ought to marry her and treat her right. At other times he felt just as certain she was just another women to please him in bed when he felt the need and that it would be the worst mistake to let himself think seriously about her. When he felt this way, he tried to get away from her as he had last night.

"Baby, I'm going out to the precinct to see if they've got any word on Pop. I'll be back soon."

"Okay, James Lee."

She had come around the bed and kissed him, keeping her lips against his so long that he felt he was being smothered. Then gently he had pulled away and gone down the stairs.

He really had meant to come back, he told himself, because it was the first night of her week's vacation. Essie had begged and pleaded with her employer in White Plains, Mrs. Ornstein, for the week off. Finally Essie had to threaten to quit before Mrs. Ornstein gave in. She had been excited about spending a whole week with James Lee, and he had felt good about it, too. But once they were in the room together he knew he would have to get away, at least for a little while. The strange thing about it was that of all the women he saw regularly, Essie was the only one who made him feel that way.

After leaving her he walked over to Bank's Bar & Grill, where he ran into Jacky and Harold. These were his two closest friends from high-school days. Now Harold was married and lived out in Long Island, and Jacky led the life of a Harlem sportsman. They only saw one another occasionally. Their meeting by accident certainly called for a celebration. At the beginning James Lee kept telling himself he should go back to Essie, but this seemed less and less important as the night went on. This morning he remembered only disconnected conversation, jumbled fragments of voices ordering gin, soda, ice, and—what was the crazy concoction that woman had been drinking?—oh, yes, Scotch, milk, and sugar.

"Send the ladies another round and ask them if we may join their party." This was Jacky speaking to the waiter at The Vet's Club. Jacky was always tailored in the best and seemed to have money to spend. He said he earned his money singing, but James Lee did not believe this because Jacky's few engagements in small Harlem night clubs never lasted for more than a week or two.

The women were picked up. They were not goodtime girls and were so embarrassed Jacky had to work overtime getting them to relax.

"No kidding. You're really from Georgia?"

"Sure we are. What's wrong with that?"

"I told you guys, didn't I? I said, 'There's a Georgia gal if I've ever seen one.' "

"Aw, go on, man. Did he, sure enough?"

"He sure did." This was Harold, who was anxious to say something to prove that he was a regular fellow, which he was not. Harold was the most successful of the three. He had a job as a layout man with an advertising firm downtown. What was it *Ebony* magazine had said in their spread on him?

TALENT AND ABILITY

SMASH COLOR BAR

"That's right," Harold was saying now, " 'there's a Georgia gal, fellas,' he said."

"How'd you know?"

" 'Cause of that evil look on your face," said Jacky. "Everybody knows that Georgia women are evil as hell."

"I knew you were lying. I told these girls, I said, 'There's a man who was born lying. We better leave him alone.' "

"Let's have a drink."

"What're you having?"

"Tom Collins. I'm hot."

"Me too. Gimme the same thing."

"And you? What are you drinking, pretty?"

"Scotch, milk, and sugar, handsome."

"I told you those Georgia gals were crazy."

"Girl, why don't you stop showing off?"

"You drink what you want. I drink what I want." She winked at James Lee, who so far had not said much. He winked back and decided she was fairly attractive.

"Waiter!"

"How do you girls happen to be out on a Sunday night? Don't tell me you're playgirls."

"We all went to the ballgame today and decided to make a night of it."

"Who do you pull for?"

"Dodgers, naturally. We all pull for the Dodgers."

"If you ask me, they've got too many spooks on that team. It'll never work out. I used to pull for Brooklyn before they got all those Negroes on the team. Then I switched to the Yanks. You know Negroes never can work together."

The women protested. "Man, you talk crazy all the time, don't you?"

"He looks colored but he talks cracker."

"I ain't kidding. I was out at Ebbets Field the other day and so many boots came running out on the diamond I went to the gate and got my money back."

The woman named Bernice pushed her chair back and stood up. "I ain't gonna sit here and listen to all this nonsense."

"Come on, girl. Have a drink. I'm just kidding. I'm a Brooklyn fan myself. Jackie Robinson is my first cousin."

Bernice sat down again. "Are you kidding? Is he sure enough?"

"Sure he is. My name is Jacky and his name is Jackie."

Everybody laughed. Bernice asked, "Why do you fellows travel around with a crackpot?"

"That's because he's got all the money," said James Lee.

"Let's go someplace else," Harold suggested.

Jacky said, "Drink up, girls. I know a jumping joint on Hundred-twenty-third Street. Drink up. Life is short, you know."

They paired off easily. James Lee found himself with the woman called Lottie. She was past thirty and seemed shapely, with high pointed breasts that pushed against him when they sat together in the taxi. The more he drank, the more he thought about them. Later, in her bedroom, her ample figure seemed almost liquid, dissolving and spreading when she loosened her girdle. By then he was drunk and, in a feeble sort of way, desperate to relieve himself sexually. Seeing her flabby breasts sagging on an overripe figure was only a momentary disappointment. Briefly he pictured Essie's animal young suppleness, but he pushed the thought away. Here was another woman to be had in another stuffy little bedroom.

"You're different, you know that?" She snapped off the light and lay beside him.

"What do you mean, different?" He was almost

gruff. He wanted to get it over with. He did not want to talk.

"The way you look, for instance. Like you're thinking hard about something. And you don't talk much. That's what I mean, different. Like the Scotch, milk, and sugar I drink. I don't even like the stuff, but it makes me different, see?"

"Yeah."

"Everybody ought to have something that sets them apart. But not too much. I'm talking crazy, I bet. That's 'cause I'm scared. Here, feel my heart."

"Come on," he said.

She smelled of sweat and powder. In the dark her flabby ugliness made no difference. He gave himself to the situation, punished himself, going beyond the few feeble exertions he felt capable of, and, completely spent and disgusted with himself and relieved only by the knowledge that the stupid night was almost over, finally fell asleep.

Luckily he awoke early and was able to avoid the embarrassment that always followed these quick affairs—the strained familiarity, the half-hearted promises to see each other again, the saying good-by to a stranger.

Outside, daylight was just coming to Harlem. There was no need now to rush to Essie. He would need time to think of a good excuse. He had found himself walking near the One-hundred-and-

thirty-fifth-Street precinct station when he decided
to go in and inquire about Hubert.

Now, on his way downtown, he wished he
could remain forever where he was, at the front
of the subway train staring ahead into the tunnel.
Its blackness was relieved only by the small red,
green, and yellow signal lights that dotted the
passageway. Perhaps if he stared into the darkness long enough he would find a way out of the
dark confusion of his life. But the tunnel suddenly burst into the brilliant black-and-white-
checkered Columbus Circle station. The Eighth
Avenue "A" train roared to a halt. Its doors hissed
open and the passengers pushed out. James Lee
turned his back to the engineer's booth, scratched
himself energetically, then squeezed through the
doorway and hurried toward the station exit.

"That's him," said James Lee.

Yes, of course he knew the little brown man
with the sleep-red eyes and the wrinkled suit. This
was his father, the queer duck of One hundred
and twenty-sixth Street.

But, thought James Lee, I don't really know
him, not really. When James Lee was very small,
in the beginning, there were the three of them in
what was called a family. But his father had never
been a part of them. He was the man who came
home to their little apartment, came home from

stores, shops, and poolrooms, and talked dreams as they ate their dinner. "This is only for a little while," he was always saying. "Just steppingstones on our way to bigger and better things."

The most persistent memory James Lee had of his earliest years was his father's shrill, hope-charged voice insisting that nothing around them was real and permanent. They were always on their way to a place where there were no railroad flats with greasy walls and piss-smelling hallways. This was a place where there was money, good food, and plenty of room to move around in. This was always coming next month, next year. Soon. These had all been lies. James Lee had understood that for a long time now. The railroad flats with the greasy walls and stinking hallways were all very real. Only Hubert Cooley was unreal. James Lee could identify him as his father, but beyond this Hubert did not exist for his son. They were strangers and had always been so.

"Don't he know," this new police sergeant was saying, "that he can get into trouble hanging around neighborhoods where he don't belong? Suppose something had happened there last night —a robbery, burglary, rape, or something? First thing we do is pick up all the loafers in the neighborhood."

James Lee told the sergeant that his father had never before been in any kind of trouble with the police and that he was certain Hubert would not loaf in the parks any more. The sergeant grumbled to himself, opened a large rectangular book, and began writing. After a few moments he paused and glared at Hubert.

"You wanna tell me your name now?"

Hubert mumbled his name. The sergeant's face was suddenly red with anger. His rock-hard voice roared at the little man. "Speak up, you! What's the matter? Can't you talk?"

Hubert took a deep breath, cleared his throat, and spoke again. "My name is Hubert Cooley."

Where did Hubert live? Where did he work, and what did he do there?

"I'm super of the building."

"What building? The one where you live?"

"Yes, and three more on the same block."

"Well, why didn't you tell me that in the first place? What am I supposed to do—read your mind?"

When the sergeant had received all the answers he wanted, he slammed the book shut, pushed it to the corner of his desk, and glared at Hubert.

"Don't you people have enough trouble without looking for it?" He pointed a thick, stubby finger. "Now hear me. If I ever catch you loafing around here again I'm gonna see that you get some time. You can believe that." He was a heavy-set man, strongly built, not yet fifty. His steel-gray hair was clipped short and added to the impression of blunt strength. His voice boomed, his slate-gray Irish eyes threatened. It was as if he personally had been insulted and at the slightest provocation would leap across the five feet of desk and railing, catch the little Negro by his scrawny neck, and snap it.

"Now get the hell out of here," he growled. Hubert turned and walked from the building. James Lee followed.

"Pop, I hope you're going right home."

"Sure, I'm going home." Hubert was examining his reflection in a restaurant window. He set his tie right and then began buttoning his vest.

"Mama's been worried about you."

"She's always worried about one thing or the other."

Hubert finished buttoning his jacket and his vest. "A man ain't got the right to sit on a park bench any more, you know that?"

"I knew that before, Pop, and so did you."

Hubert changed the subject. "You got any money?"

"Why?"

"I need it for something," Hubert snapped. "Let me have five dollars until payday."

James Lee knew that Hubert disliked having to ask him for money and it made James Lee uncomfortable. His first urge was to give his father what he wanted so that the scene would be over as quickly as possible. But nothing annoyed him more than his father's expensive habit of playing the numbers. To James Lee the numbers game thrived on mass ignorance, and, though he might occasionally gamble at poker or dice, he had never chanced a nickel on the long odds of the numbers. Besides, his father's payday never came. His mother had begun to collect the small superintendent's salary. That was the only way she could be certain any of the bills would be paid.

James Lee took some silver from his pocket. "Here's fifty cents to get uptown with, Pop. This is the best I can do."

Hubert did not move. "I'll pay you the five dollars on payday."

James Lee fought down a desire to snatch one of the two bills from his pocket and give it to Hubert. But good money was good money and there was no sense in throwing it away. Besides, he would probably have to buy Essie a present to pacify her. This little man, the crazy fool! Why couldn't he be like everybody else.

"Nothing doing, Pop."

Without another word Hubert turned and walked toward the Eighth Avenue subway. For all his neatness, he was a shabby figure. James Lee returned the silver to his pocket. He had no urge to go after Hubert. He would call his mother and tell her his father was coming.

He felt as if his clothes were sticking to his body. He wanted a bath and a change of clothing, but first he would have to rush over to the garage. Suppose that dispatcher had given his taxi to someone else? He couldn't afford to lose a day's work. After picking up the cab he would rush home to Essie. He stopped at the corner and caught a crosstown bus.

4

In the room on One hundred and twenty-fourth
Street Essie Dee Turner tried going back to sleep
but her nerves were tense. A few minutes earlier
Essie had been shocked out of her sleep by the
shrill scream of a woman. She had sat straight up
in her bed, wide awake, not daring to breathe.
Then the woman had started crying, a low, throaty
moan, and Essie had realized with relief that it

was not a woman who had screamed but only that doggoned cat out there in the back yard. She was certain it was the same cat that raised so much sand every time she spent a night here. The good Lord knew, that old pussy would cause her to have heart failure one of these nights if she kept screaming like that.

She lay back on her pillow and tried to get to sleep. Where was James Lee? Could something have happened to him? As she thought about him it seemed that he was there, lying beside her, touching his lips to her ears and throat, murmuring all that foolish talk that always made her wonder if he was sincere. It was: Baby, you know I love you, don't you, honey? I'm crazy about you. You kill me with those crazy eyes. . . . New York nonsense talk, she called it, but she liked to hear it. Yes, James Lee, sweet black man . . . he had her number, all right. The tension lifted. She yawned and fell asleep.

They were somewhere, the two of them, inside a house. She knew this house well and felt at home here. James Lee said something about being sleepy and she agreed that it was time to go to bed. She watched him take off his clothes, felt that same anxious sensation she always experienced when she saw the hardness of his body. And she saw that he was not really sleepy; nor, come to think of it, was she. They were together as one, she and James Lee, making love in that wild, clutching, fighting way that usually left her weak and trembling. But it was not definite to her, and she was vaguely dissatisfied.

And now they were in a living room. She could see this very clearly. The light-colored furniture was very modern, like Mrs. Ornstein's in White Plains. It was not cheap, either, not the kind they sell on One hundred and twenty-fifth Street, but solid stuff she would take good care of and polish each and every day.

And there were children. She could not really see them, but she knew they were there. Perhaps they were a boy and a girl or two boys or two girls. She was not certain of anything except that they belonged to her and James Lee. They were all over the place, those kids, running and giggling and making a racket, and James Lee was smiling all over himself because he really did like them, after all. Well, hadn't she been telling him all along that kids were the best things in the world? Essie had so much happiness that everything was soft and warm.

Then she saw the basin and she was living through the whole terrible episode again. That basin! She would never forget it, never! That was her blood, wasn't it, the pinkish splotches on the white enamel? At first she was not certain, but it had to be her blood because it was she who sat over the basin. It was strange to be looking at it like that. The pain was there, too, the one that was sharper than any other, deeper than any other; the one that made her go hot and cold and finally numb. It had been awful, terrible. God Jesus! there had been no words for it. She had felt the pain even in her teeth.

That damned woman! The wiry, mannish little woman that looked no more like a nurse than she looked like the Queen of Sheba. She was there, this woman, on her knees in front of Essie, probing with the long metal thing, scraping and murmuring: "It won't be long, honey, just a little more." But suddenly it wasn't the little ugly woman down there but James Lee, and Essie knew that it had been James Lee all the time. The hot pain was pulling at her spine and throbbing at the base of her neck. She heard the scream that was torn out of her body and she was thinking: Oh, Lord, Lord, please. I can't stand it, please, Lord! She pulled at James Lee's head and struck her fists against his shoulders. Please, honey, this ain't the way it's supposed to be. James Lee, baby, it was never meant to be this way. Can't you see? Please, please! She pulled at him, struck him, pleaded with him, but he kept right on. There, in her pain, she saw how terrible everything was, how wrong and awful to kill the baby that wasn't born, and if this was the way it was supposed to be, then they were better off dead. She had to stop it before it was too late. She had to stand up and fight a thing like that or there was no hope for anybody. She felt herself drowning, being sucked down into the heavy blackness, and her throat was clogged with a terror. She opened her mouth to scream but no sound came. She was lost.

Again Essie was sitting straight up in the bed. Her breath came in deep, noisy gasps. Her body was wet with perspiration and she trembled with cold. Her eyes were wide open and unseeing. She wanted to get out of the bed, but she could not will her arms and legs to move.

Above, on the next landing, she could hear heavy footsteps moving along the squeaky wooden floors of the hallway. This meant that it was seven-thirty and the plump, brown-skinned woman up-stairs, the one that always reminded Essie of her mother down home, was getting her husband off to work before she left herself.

The woman's soprano voice seeped through the thin floors. "Lonzo, don't you forget to go by and see how Leo is."

Essie knew that Lonzo was about forty-five years old and baldheaded with a bulging pot of a belly. He said, "Woman, if you was to stop worry-ing about what *I* is supposed to do, and worried about what *you* is supposed to do, you'd be a damned sight better off."

"Lonzo!" Her high voice was full of shock. "Don't be cursing in the hallway like that so every-body in the world can hear how evil you are."

Now Lonzo was down to Essie's landing. He was mumbling to himself as he walked past her door. "With that woman, if it ain't one thing it's the other." Essie heard him sigh wearily as he started to let himself down the next flight of stairs.

The talk had served to pry her mind and body loose from the grip of the nightmare. She began to think. Quietly and slowly the thought formed itself: I've got to get out of here. Calmly and soberly it took body and grew. *I've got to get out of here.*

Still she did not move, and now her eyes darted from the dirty, streaked wall in front of her and swept around the room. They rested a moment on the black, greasy gas stove that she had scrubbed and scoured with steel wool and had never been able to clean; sped on to the single window that looked out onto the nothingness of other back windows with the same torn green shades and the gray grassless yards below; darted up to the dingy ceiling and stopped on the large heavy white patch of plaster that she had told James Lee would one day crash down and kill them.

I've got to get out of here.

She had never liked the room, not from that very first moment when James Lee had swung open the door and announced that this was it. He had done this proudly, as if he had accomplished something in finding it. Yes, a young couple needed a place of their own. Each time they went to a hotel she was nervous and tense because she realized the clerk and all the hotel help knew that she and James Lee were not married. James Lee had said this was the way people did things in New York, but that did not make her feel any better. So she had agreed to the room. But this place was much too small, hardly large enough for the roaches, let alone her and James Lee. Why, the room she had in the Ornstein house in White Plains was fully twice as large. Of course, it was in the basement of somebody else's home, but even that was better than having to walk up four flights of stairs through a dimly lit hallway to this dirty little back room.

Essie's body trembled under the nightgown. It was silly to be so cold when anybody could see that it was going to be another hot day. *I've got to get out of here.* But still she did not move.

Despite her dislike for the room, their first night had gone well. They laughed about how much noise the bed made and decided to get some lubricating oil so that everybody in the house would not know their business. James Lee declared that the last couple must have been pretty old if they hadn't minded such noisy bedsprings. Later in the night, after they had given to and taken from each other, after they were both drowsy and satisfied and ready for sleep, Essie had gone to the bureau drawer and taken out her nightgown. What the hell was that? James Lee wanted to know. She answered that it did not seem right to sleep naked, and he laughed so hard that Essie was certain he would wake everybody in the building. She had to kiss him on the mouth to shut him up, and later they slept, her head on his chest, their bodies warm against each other, and the nightgown on the chair, where she had left it.

She forced herself to concentrate: I've got to get out of here.

Now she moved for the first time, pushing back the covers and throwing her legs over the side of the bed. With her toes she found her bedroom slippers and slid her feet into them. She jerked her robe from the chair and wrapped it around her trembling body as she stood up.

Who did James Lee think she was, anyway? He certainly had his people confused. If he thought she was going to sit there like a fool and wait for him to make up his mind to come home, he had another think coming. After pleading with old lady Ornstein for these few days off just so she could spend some time with this good-for-nothing, low-down snake of a Negro—did he think she was going to spend those days sitting in their dirty room alone? Well, we would see about that!

Her pink toothbrush lay on the bureau in the glass container beside the tube of toothpaste. She picked them up and gathered her washcloth, towel, and soap from the bureau drawer. She pulled her robe tightly about her and cracked the door to see if there was anyone in the hallway. Finding it empty, she pulled the door shut behind her and tiptoed along the hallway toward the bathroom. But just then a man came down the stairs from the floor above, a light-skinned young man with a round porkpie hat. He smiled—she thought it was more of a grin—and said good morning to her. She only half nodded and hurried to the bathroom, where she locked herself inside. When these New York men spoke to you they were usually after something more than a good morning. None of them had any respect for women. Why, even married men had tried to get fresh with her! She splashed cold water over her face and shivered.

New York men were no good anyway, Essie reflected. She had gone through the works with one by name of James Lee Cooley and he was the last one she ever would have. If anybody ever saw her going with another New York man, trying to fall in love or do something foolish like that, she wanted that somebody to give her a good swift kick.

Now she was hurrying frantically. She had to get dressed and away before James Lee came. If he were to come in just now . . . well, she had let him change her mind before.

In her haste she dropped the toothbrush container and its thin glass tinkled over the floor.

Impatiently scooping it up, she pricked her hand with a crystalline fragment. She said "Shoot!", and flung the debris into the trash basket.

Back in the room, she looked at the reflection of her slender brown legs in the mirror as she stepped into her skirt. Her thighs were lean and smooth, and she told herself for the thousandth time that she could use a few more pounds around the hips. But then, New York girls liked being skinny. New York . . . James Lee . . . maybe he could push these local girls around, but he was thinking like Grandpa dreamed if he had any idea he could do that to her. Men were crazy. All you had to do was let one of them know you liked him a little bit, and right off he . . . how did the song go?

> . . . *he'll start cutting a hog.*
> *Just be good to a man, Lord,*
> *And he'll treat you like a dog . . .*

She sat down before the mirror and began brushing her hair with quick, angry strokes. The ends were breaking off, and it was time to have it done again. Maybe when she got to her sister's house she would call Madam Johnson's for an appointment. But why not splurge a bit? Yes, it would not be Madam Johnson's this time but Rose Meta's. A good hairdo would pick up her spirits.

Suddenly the hand with the brush stopped in mid-air. She wasn't coming back! She had not really known it until that moment, but it was clear now. It was not just another of those times when he would melt her with a smile or a kiss. It was not just that he had left her alone on the first night of her vacation. Worst things had happened between them and she had walked out only to return at the first telephone call. But this was different.

So there was no hurry now. It no longer made any difference if he came in before she left. She knew he could not stop her leaving. He could get down on his knees, start cursing and threatening, even try to make love to her, but he would not be able to stop her.

She felt really happy, and it seemed to her that this happiness was a new feeling altogether. She looked into the mirror and said aloud, "Essie Dee Turner, you're a damned fool." And she thought, Excuse me, Jesus, for talking like that. When she finished her make-up she began throwing things into her suitcase. She would take only what was necessary. The rest she could get later.

She slammed the door behind her. Inside, something fell to the floor with a dull crash—probably the water glass that had been setting on the basin. Even this made her feel good. For a moment she toyed with the idea of going back and smashing everything she could get her hands on. But now she wanted to be outside the house altogether. Walking down the steps, she hoped she would

meet old lady Graham on the first floor. Mrs.
Graham was the landlady from Barbados who always looked at Essie Dee as if she knew the girl
was living in sin. One thing was certain: if she
stuck her head into the hallway this morning,
she would get a piece of Essie's mind. But old
lady Graham, perhaps sensing danger, did not appear. Essie opened the door and stepped into the
street.

The loudspeaker of the record shop at the corner was giving out with a hot record by a white
woman who sounded almost colored:

> *Going to Chicago, sorry I can't take you,*
> *Going to Chicago, sorry I can't take you,*
> *Nothing up there a man like you can do.* *

Essie decided that one day she would buy that
record just to remind her of the day she broke
free of James Lee.

She stopped at the corner of Lenox Avenue to
change her bag from one hand to the other, and
that was when the man bumped into her. He
bowed slightly and tipped his hat and said, "Excuse me, Miss." He had a pencil mustache and he
was grinning. Essie was sure he had bumped into
her on purpose.

"Can I help you with your bag, Miss?" He still

* From "Goin' To Chicago Blues" by James Rushing and
Count Basie. Copyright © 1941 by Bregman, Vocco and Conn,
Inc., 1619 Broadway, New York 19, New York. Used by per-
mission.

held his hat in his hand and showed a wide expanse of teeth.

"Look, joker," yelled Essie, "the way I feel about men this morning, you'd better get the hell out of my face!"

She had shouted at him so suddenly and so loudly she had frightened herself. The man's grin disappeared and he pushed his hat hastily onto his head. "Excuse me, Miss," he whispered and walked quickly toward One hundred and twenty-fifth Street.

Imagine cursing out loud like that! Why, she was beginning to sound just like one of those New York girls.

She raised her hand and hailed a taxi going south on the other side of Lenox. But a taxi going north was closer, and he gassed his car toward the curb where Essie stood. The driver making the U turn saw himself about to lose a fare and he put on a burst of speed. Their tires squealed as they slammed on brakes to avoid a collision. Essie walked around the intruding taxi and stepped into the one she had hailed.

That would really have been something, she thought, if the two cabs had run into each other trying to get to me. What in the world was the matter with her, thinking all these devilish thoughts and yelling at men in the street? She sat back on the seat and crossed her legs and smiled. You could say what you wanted about Essie Dee

Turner, that she was not the smartest person in the world, that it sometimes took her a while to catch on; but one thing was sure: she never made the same mistake twice. Nobody could say that about Mrs. Turner's little girl.

5

This morning Gertrude Cooley told herself that she had too much to do to worry about Hubert. Monday was trash collection day, and all the cans would have to be out on the street before ten o'clock. In the house next door they were complaining about having no hot water, and she would have to get the furnace started. This was not an easy job once the fire died completely. A pane was broken in the front door of number 67 across the street and would have to be replaced. Sarah Anderson was complaining that her toilet would not flush, but this would have to wait until Hubert came back. She couldn't be expected to do everything.

She prepared bacon, eggs, hominy grits, and coffee for herself. She always ate a good breakfast before beginning her morning chores. When she had finished, she put the dirty dishes in the sink and covered them with water. A good meal for the roaches, she thought, but this morning she did not have time to skirmish with them. For seventeen years in this apartment she had been at war with the roaches, but they seemed as plentiful as ever. She sighed. Despite all the powders and sprays and the efforts to starve them out by keeping the kitchen clean and dry, it looked as if they would win in the end. "You'll bury me yet," she murmured, taking a halfhearted whack at a black peanut shape that scooted for refuge into a hole under the sink.

Gertrude put on her work clothes. These consisted of a green fatigue jacket and trousers James Lee had brought home from the army, which she had altered so they fitted her. She was a tall, heavy woman, big-bosomed, with strong arms and shoulders. Her movements seemed slow, but this was because they were so deliberate. The average task took less time in her hands. At almost fifty years of age she was in good health, though in the last few years she had begun to tire more quickly.

She went down to the basement and brought up two cans of trash. This was difficult, because the cans were large and heavy and she had to drag them up one step at a time. It was really a man's work, she told herself, and she ought not to be straining her back with heavy cans. But the job had to be done, and if Hubert was not there it was up to her to do it. James Lee helped occasionally, but he was not home much. Nowadays he often stayed away all night. She did not mind this. He had a right to his life without having to worry about the old folks. But she wished someone would see that she had some rights, too. Both her men, Hubert and James Lee, ought to understand that she could not keep up a house by herself.

She dragged the last of the cans to the front vestibule, where she paused to catch her breath. She would like to die, sudden-like, while they were both away from home. She could imagine their faces as they stood above her body. Maybe they would cry a little—not for her, but because they had treated her so badly and now they would not have anybody to wash, clean, and cook for them. It would serve them right.

She took a deep breath and began dragging the first can down to the street. It was not like Gertrude to indulge in morbid thoughts. She never worried about death and sickness. Besides, she knew that if she did pass on, they would not really care. James Lee might think he had loved his poor old mother, but neither he nor Hubert knew anything about love. Loving somebody was doing things for them and helping to make life easier for them. Clearly, nobody loved Gertrude.

"Good morning, Mrs. Cooley."

"Good morning, Mrs. Williams."

Mrs. Williams was a decrepit old widow who lived across the street. Her yellow, lifeless skin sagged on her bones and her trembling face always looked as if she were about to cry. She lived alone in her little third-floor front room with the idea that a mysterious group of people was planning to kill her. This same group had been responsible for her husband's death fifteen years before. Like many people in the block, she found Gertrude a sympathetic listener, and every few days brought in new evidence she had uncovered.

"It won't be long now, Mrs. Cooley."

"It won't?"

"Oh, no, indeed," Mrs. Williams whispered. Gertrude detected the odor of the cheap wine Mrs. Williams drank. It was a sweet, heavy smell, oppressive and sad.

"Any day now, Mrs. Cooley," she said. "In fact, you might say any minute."

"What are you going to do about it?" Gertrude asked. About this same time the previous year Mrs. Williams had felt she was in immediate danger. At other times she felt she had her enemies stymied. Gertrude had no idea what caused the old woman to feel one way and then the other, but it was obvious that all of Mrs. Williams' fantasies were very real to her. This morning Gertrude was slightly annoyed. She had troubles and complaints of her own. She wished she could bring herself to be rude to Mrs. Williams, but she could not.

"I ain't afraid of them, Mrs. Cooley. You know that, don't you?" Gertrude nodded. Mrs. Williams' deep-lined face seemed to grow duller even as Gertrude was looking at it. "But this time I think they will win, just the way they did with Mr. Williams." She rested her hand on Gertrude's arm. "God bless you, dear Mrs. Cooley. You're the only one that understands." And with her odor of sweet wine and lace, with her petticoat showing beneath the hem of her dress, Mrs. Williams walked across the street to her little room with its quiet terror.

Gertrude went back to work. What was it like, she wondered, to be like Mrs. Williams, to think about unreal things as if they actually existed? Gertrude counted herself among the lucky ones of the world in that she was practical and down to earth. Everyone who knew her shared this opinion. She did not think of herself as especially bright. She had no idea what made the world tick, nor did she much care. But she looked upon herself as strong. She felt a measure of pride when friends said to her: "Gertrude, I declare, girl, don't nothing ever get you down, does it?"

No, nothing ever did. It was almost two years now since she had discovered that Hubert really intended to leave her. One day she had decided to clean his closet, and inside, pushed back into a corner, she had found the suitcase. Even now she could remember the smell of its new leather. She had never seen it before, had not known it was in the house. Under a transparent plastic covering were shirts, ties, socks, and underwear, all new. Certainly an ordinary thing, a suitcase with clothing, but when she thought of the hints and innuendoes, the veiled threats—"Woman, you just might wake up one of these mornings and find me long gone"—the suitcase and the clothing, hidden for she did not know how long, made sense to her as soon as she discovered them.

In the cellar of the house next door she began to gather kindling and paper for the furnace. Whenever Hubert wandered away and let the fire go out, she had to get it started again. The draft of the old furnace was not good. When she set fire to the paper and kindling the cellar filled up with smoke. With stinging eyes, coughing and wheezing, she stooped over the door of the furnace and tried to nurse the tiny flame within. This was also a man's job, she decided, and she was beginning to think she was the only man in the house.

No, she never let anything get her down. She had never mentioned finding the suitcase in the closet, nor had he brought it up, though he knew she must have seen it. It was a silent barrier between them. Well, Gertrude, she told herself, you're pretty good. You wake up one morning and find you don't have any marriage, that the old man don't want you any more, but you just keep on going like nothing ever happened.

Oh, she had known before that everything was not all right. She had her ways of telling. It was before the discovery of the suitcase, almost a year before, that they had tried for love in bed. She had sought to arouse in him a need, a desire for her, and he had made an effort to respond; but nothing had come of it, nothing but embarrassment and escape to opposite sides of the bed and heavy, forced sleep.

The color of the fire changed from a dull yellow to an intense blue and the smoke began to clear away. She closed the door and set the thermostat. Then she went to her apartment and washed her face. Her work was not half done and she was tired already. She looked at herself in the mirror and saw that she was ugly. Not at first, of course, but gradually, as she was able to imagine what *he* saw when *he* looked. Yes, she was ugly. She swallowed hard and turned away from the glass. "To tell you the truth," she said aloud, "he ain't so hot-looking either."

Sometimes it was almost too much to bear, the dry, empty routine with its frustration: waking, eating and sleeping, working four apartment houses, going to church. "I'm forty-nine years old!" she said, thinking: Lord, only forty-nine, not old at all. She felt she was brimming over with life and she wanted to give everything of herself. She was hurt that nobody wanted her—not Hubert, not anybody. So she kept herself strong. When she felt a need to be needed, loved, made over, she teased herself and said, "You're not a hot girl any more, so keep your pants on." And sometimes she managed to laugh.

Where was she to blame? During the past three dull and empty years she had re-examined every particle of their lives together so that she would know where she had failed. But the most intense remembering, the going over in her mind of everything that had passed between them—all this had uncovered nothing to clear away her confusion.

She opened the supply closet and took out a pane of glass that would fit into the front door of Sixty-seven. With the glass, the tools, and the putty she crossed the street.

"Jesus, have mercy!" she muttered, and she meant have mercy on Hubert and James Lee and

Gertrude Cooley. God knew she had done the best she could.

She had stuck with him through all the hard years. At the time they married, Hubert worked as a messenger in the garment district. He liked his job and his boss, Mr. Rosenblatt, who taught Hubert the value of cloth, how to measure and cut it. Hubert was a hard worker and thrifty. He began saving his money because he wanted to open a dress shop in Harlem. But Mr. Rosenblatt was forced to shut down in 1932, and Hubert was out of work for a while. He used up his savings before he found another job. In 1934, Hubert rented a grocery store and managed to hold onto it for a year before it went under. In 1936, he rented another one, smaller and less ambitious, but this failed, too. Between these ventures he worked at anything he could find and saved until he could try again. Later there was a poolroom that was always crowded but never seemed to show a profit, and soon that had to be given up.

These were the lean thirties, bad thirties—the furious years of struggling just for food and a place to live. On gray, hopeless mornings Gertrude often sat on the "slave block." That was what colored women called the little park up in the Bronx where they were scrutinized by the white housewives who decided which ones looked honest and clean enough for a day's work in their homes. Gertrude was chosen often enough, but when she was away she had to leave James Lee alone. Each night she rushed home, cleaned, cooked, and laid out dinner for them. The boy, always dark and silent, would eat hungrily while Hubert talked away about how much money they had saved and how long it would be before they could lease the store or shop and go into business for themselves again. But somehow things never worked out the way he said they would.

The best thing of all happened in 1938. This was when she heard about the superintendent's job on One hundred and twenty-sixth Street. A job like that meant always having a roof over their heads and being able to draw a small salary besides. James Lee was ten years old that year, and it was time they were settling down in one place. At first Hubert had not understood how important it was. They quarreled about it, but gradually he came around. One day he walked down to Madison Avenue and talked with Reisling & Sons, Real Estate Agents. He came home with the job. For fifteen years now they had had an apartment rent free and always enough to eat.

It was a little past eight o'clock when Hubert came home.

"That you, Hubert?"

"It's me, Gertrude."

She made a vow. She would not argue with him. She would not start a fight and if one started she would not keep it up. What did it really matter that he had been away from home two days? What was wrong between them was deeper than that. She would do her best to keep everything calm. Nothing was going to get her down. She went out to the hallway where he was taking off his jacket and hanging it in the closet.

He said, "Gonna be hot today."

"Looks that way."

"How you feel?"

"Fine," she answered.

He did not look at her.

"James Lee call you?"

"Yes."

He said, "I spent the night in jail, y'know."

"I hear tell."

"Colored man can't even sit in the park no more."

He began unbuttoning his shirt. He was methodical and neat. She liked to watch his movements. Once the shirt was off he would find a hanger, put the shirt on it, and fasten all the buttons before hanging it in the closet. It did not matter that the shirt was dirty. Hubert did not believe in crumpling shirts into a ball and stuffing them into a hamper.

"You hungry?" asked Gertrude.

"Some."

"I'm fixing you some breakfast."

"Thanks."

After Hubert had taken a bath and shaved he came into the kitchen and sat down to the food she had prepared. He emptied his plate and asked for more.

"Did the trash get out all right?"

"Uh-huh. I put it out."

"Sorry I stayed away like that." Hubert spoke gruffly. This was an apology.

"That's all right." She sat down at the table and watched him eat.

"I like four-seventeen today. Dreamed it last night just as clear as anything."

She said, "Sounds all right." Gertrude sometimes played but never for more than a few pennies. Since Hubert had begun to bet so much on the numbers she did not like to think about them. They were silent for a while.

Suddenly Hubert said, "Do we have any money, Gertrude?"

"There's only seven dollars in the whole house. Just enough for the gas and light bill." Almost involuntarily she asked why.

"Oh, nothing," Hubert mumbled. "If we don't have it, we don't have it." He shrugged and went on with his breakfast.

When he had finished he asked Gertrude what work had to be done. She showed him the pad on which she scribbled the complaints of the tenants.

They decided which ones should be taken care of first, and Hubert went out.

He worked diligently. He unclogged Sarah Anderson's toilet and stoked all the furnaces. He swept and mopped the hallways of 67 and then spackled over cracks that had developed in the plaster. He set traps, he painted, he hammered, he sawed. Hubert Cooley was absolutely the busiest house superintendent in Harlem that morning until eleven-thirty. That was when Gertrude left the apartment to go to the store. Hubert took this opportunity to slip into the bedroom and pry open her bureau drawer. He took out the seven dollars designated for the gas and electric bills. With the money tucked snugly in his pocket, he hurried away down the street.

6

The one person in the whole world Iretha did not want to see this morning was her kid sister Essie. They got along together well enough, but Essie always chose Iretha's busiest days to come bursting in. On Mondays her schedule was always crowded, and today was no exception. At nine-thirty she had a beauty appointment at Rose Meta's that she simply could not break. Then she

would have to rush back to the apartment, because
at noon Lillian Sommerville, Dr. Sommerville's sister, was dropping by to discuss Iretha's candidacy
for membership in the Wheatley Social Circle.
This was the charity group that gave some of Harlem's most important social affairs and collected
money for the poor little children in the West In-
dies. Also, sometime today Iretha would have to
sit down and write a letter of resignation from The
Fun Girls, that silly little club she had joined years
before, when she had worked as a practical nurse
at Harlem Hospital. Some of the members were
bound to say she felt she had outgrown The Fun
Girls, but that would not bother Iretha. She knew
how they were—nasty, like crabs, pulling one another down. Goodness, she did have a lot to do!
Tonight she and her husband Hugh were going to
the theater. Trummy Carpenter, the well-known
lawyer who was expecting a magistrate's appointment if the November elections worked out as expected, had given Iretha and Hugh tickets for the
Broadway musical hit *Guys and Dolls*, which
meant that Iretha would have to arrange for a
baby sitter. It was really very thoughtless of Essie
to come visiting at eight-thirty in the morning.

She knew it was Essie by the three short, insist-
ent rings. Essie never came visiting except when
she had had an argument with James Lee. She
would moon around the house crying all morning, getting in Iretha's way and upsetting the chil-

dren. Then James Lee would call, and Essie would go running back like a tamed puppy. Iretha resolved that today she would not listen to any of Essie's tearful stories. If the girl was silly enough to run around with low-class Negroes, she deserved all the trouble she was having.

Iretha had an impulse not to push the buzzer that would open the door five flights below. Maybe Essie would go away. Yes, that was it! She would not answer the bell. But she felt a tinge of guilt. After all, Essie was her sister, unsophisticated and naïve, it was true, but her sister nevertheless.

Down below, Essie pushed the bell again, three short, compelling rings.

"Oh, darn," muttered Iretha. She pressed the buzzer and bit her lower lip as she waited. It was as if her kid sister had read her thoughts and said, "No, no, Iretha, that wouldn't be nice." Iretha decided to tell Essie that if she had to drop by unexpectedly she must try to avoid doing it on Mondays. But Essie would be crying when she came in. Well, Iretha would wait until she had calmed down and tell her then. Iretha would be firm.

No one could accuse her of having neglected Essie. When the girl had come up from their home in Cheraw, North Carolina, Iretha and Hugh had taken her in. This was when there had hardly been room for themselves, before they moved into this larger, more modern apartment overlooking River-

side Drive. They had introduced Essie to their
friends and taken her to the Annual Christmas
Ball given by the Upper Manhattan Lawyers'
Guild in the Skyline Room of the Theresa Hotel.
Iretha had insisted on buying Essie a gown for the
affair, a white silk thing, not daring and only
vaguely suggestive. The smart set had made a fuss
over her. The young men had found one pretext
after another to come over to their table and get
themselves introduced to the new young face that
seemed slightly out of place in the colored lights
and restrained conviviality of the Skyline Room.
Iretha had felt that the triumph belonged more to
her than to Essie. She foresaw her sister making a
nice marriage with one of the young doctors or
lawyers—it did not matter who it was so long as
the man was a professional who could take good
care of Essie without her having to work. Essie
would not have the long hard struggle for security
that Iretha had had during those first years in
New York, before she married Hugh. He was not
yet forty and already was an inspector with a gold
badge at the post office. That night at the ball a
photographer from the *Amsterdam News* snapped
Essie and Ted Thayer, Jr., the son of the well-
known New Jersey real-estate man, as they
danced. The picture had been displayed promi-
nently in that Friday's paper. But in the end the
whole thing had come to nothing because Essie
was so stubborn.

Iretha sank onto her new chaise longue and lit a cigarette. There was one thing you could say about the Turner girls—meaning herself and Essie and two other sisters who still lived in the South. There was not one of them who was hard to look at. Iretha was thirty-five, but she felt she looked ten years younger. Perhaps none of them was light-complexioned, but that was a handicap which was overcome by their tall, slender figures and the teasing, chestnut brown of their skin. Iretha had always felt that the baby of the family, Essie Dee, would grow into the prettiest of them all. She had been right.

"Tsk!" She made a noise with her tongue and ground the cigarette into the ash tray. That was what made it so damned tragic. A girl had to be sharp in New York, on her toes every minute, ready to take advantage of the slightest opportunity. How she had worked to get where she was! And she had not stopped yet, not by a long shot. Any girl as pretty as Essie, with a sister who had offered to pay the bills, as Iretha had, had no business working for Jews up in Westchester. Essie was stupid and ungrateful.

When she heard the elevator door in the hallway open, Iretha uncrossed her legs, got up from the chaise, and went to the door. On her face was the smile that was always there when admitting someone to the apartment. She was hoping that Essie would not cry very long and would leave soon so that she could get back on her schedule. She was surprised to find when she opened the door that Essie stood there smiling back at her.

"Hi, baby," said Iretha.

"Hi, yourself," responded Essie.

They touched cheeks. Essie seemed so happy that Iretha asked, "Girl, are you all right?"

"Well, look at me," said Essie, spreading her arms. "Am I standing on my own two feet or am I not?"

Iretha stared. There was a twinkle in Essie's eye that puzzled her. She did not like to be confused so early in the morning.

"I'm hungry," announced Essie. She went to the kitchen and swung open the door of the refrigerator. "What you got to eat, girl? I'm starved."

Essie began to take leftovers out of the refrigerator and soon was sitting at the table eating the remains of Sunday's dinner. What in the world had got into the kid? Iretha decided that what she had seen in Essie's eyes was not a twinkle at all but a glint. Essie looked as if she were at war. Iretha lit another cigarette and continued to stare.

7

Frank's Garage was near the East River on First Avenue at One hundred and sixteenth Street, an old red-brick structure with green painted windows. There were sixty cabs and a hundred and twenty regular drivers backed up by a force of mechanics, garage helpers, and several extra drivers. Together they were supposed to keep each car on the street twenty-three hours a day.

Frank DaVini was a chunky Italian who smoked
and chewed cheap cigars and had ulcers. He never
nagged his men about averages. If a man's money
on the clock began to fall consistently below the
average, Frank would call him into the office and
ask him what was wrong. Didn't he like working
for Frank? Didn't he like having a new car to
drive? Didn't he like having a whole army of
mechanics waiting to take care of his car when it
broke down? Didn't he like coming to work in the
morning and knowing his car would be there waiting for him? Or maybe he would like to work for
one of those companies where they made the men
shape up every morning and sometimes a hackie
didn't get a car at all. Or maybe he'd like to go to
work for National and drive one of those Check-
ers, where a man couldn't make a living because
the new DeSotos like Frank's were always stealing
fares from him. Or maybe he didn't like being able
to draw his money every day instead of having to
wait until the end of the week. And having a paid
vacation for a whole week every year. Frank never
gave the hackie a chance to argue or apologize.
He would get up from his green little desk, smile,
slap the hackie on the back, and say, "All right, get
on out there and put some money on that clock."
Nobody's feelings were hurt. More often than not,
the cabbie worked harder and produced more
money. If he did not, he came in one morning and
found that his car had been given to someone else.

"Jesus Christ!" screamed Frank DaVini this morning, as if he were in pain. It was a high, shrill exclamation, almost a squeal. "What the hell is this?" He stood in the middle of the garage pointing at car number three-six-eight, the only car parked in the entire garage. Frank's outraged voice shot into every corner and reverberated off the walls.

"Danny! Danny! Goddamit! Come out here."

The mechanics at work on the second tier of the garage peeked over the railing to see what was ailing the boss. Danny O'Halloran came hurrying out of the dispatcher's office. He was a tall, blond young man, athletically built, good-looking. He did not think of himself as the best dispatcher in New York City, but he was certain that as a ladies' man he was unsurpassed. Among the drivers and the mechanics he was known as Young Genitals.

"Da-a-aneee!"

"What is it, Frank?"

Frank had not seen Danny come up. His deliberately soft, self-assured voice startled Frank. Danny always made Frank feel cold and off his stride. The syndicate that owned the greater bloc of stock in the garage had suggested Danny for the job and there had been little that Frank could do about it. On his own he would never have hired Danny. It was not just that he was too good-looking, a pretty boy, but he had never driven a hack. What kind of garage had a dispatcher who had never hacked? To Frank it was almost unethical.

"Danny, is this car in running condition?"

"Yeah, Frank, it is—"

"Then, Holy Jesus, what the hell is it doing here? It's almost nine o'clock."

"The driver isn't here yet."

"Is he the only one who can drive this friggin' car?" squealed Frank.

"You know how things are in the summer," Danny said. "There aren't too many extra men around."

"Don't hand me that. There're plenty of guys around who'd be happy to drive a new car."

"What can I do, Frank?" said Danny with a spread of his hands. "If an extra man had come in, I would have given him the car—"

"Git on the phone; call some of the old drivers; do something and git that goddamned car out of here, Danny. You hear me!" Frank walked toward his own car parked in the driveway. He took quick, short puffs from the cigar. He was being loud and authoritative, but there was also a whining note of protest so that Danny would understand there was nothing personal in what he was saying. "Is that car making any dough for you or me or anybody else while it sits here in the garage? No. Take the car away from the damn driver if he don't want it."

He opened the door of his dark blue Chrysler and got in. "Jesus Christ," he exclaimed as he slammed the door shut and started the motor. "Nine o'clock and the friggin' car sitting up here in the friggin' garage and not a friggin' thing wrong with it!" He wiped the sweat from his plump face with a handkerchief as he backed through the garage exit. "Jesus Christ!" he exclaimed again as he drove toward Second Avenue.

Danny walked back into his office. He would give Cooley hell when he came in. Who did that black bastard think he was, not even calling the office to say he would be late?

Evaline, the secretary and cashier, was seated at her typewriter. She was a brunette, petite and attractive. Danny stood behind her with his hands on her shoulders. As he talked he strained his eyes to see down the top of her low-cut blouse.

"If I get any calls, switch 'em upstairs, huh?"

Evaline continued her typing. Her voice was cold and contemptuous. "You've got to give me a rub-down to tell me that?"

He took his hands away and walked out of the office. The little bitch! He would get her yet, just for meanness, just to hear her cry. Yes, he would see that she cried. Now he would tell the grease monkeys about the virgin he had snared over the week end. He enjoyed seeing the looks of envy on the faces of those married guys when they listened to his stories. He ran a comb through his hair. Well, some guys had it and some guys didn't. He had it. Was it his fault?

James Lee's fear of being late amounted almost to a phobia. Somewhere he had heard that white folks believed Negroes always traveled behind-time, and, although he told himself he did not care what white folks thought, he always made an extra effort to be punctual where they were concerned.

As he approached the garage he felt he especially did not want to see Frank DaVini. When Frank started yelling at you, he never gave you a chance to say anything and he always made you feel that you had done him a personal injury. Even if you did not like to be yelled at, especially by white people, you could never really answer Frank because there was something in his voice that made you suspect he was halfway right in what he was saying.

On the other hand, James Lee did not mind meeting the new Irish dispatcher they had brought in. He did not like the Irish anyway, and he would never take any guff off a young punk like O'Halloran. He took the dispatch card for his car and punched the time clock.

"Hey, Cooley, wait up!"

O'Halloran's voice sounded harsh and threatening in the empty garage.

"What is it?" James Lee asked.

Danny was descending the steps from the second tier. A cigarette was in his mouth and he was lighting it as he came down. He spoke with slight irritation in his voice. "Wait up a minute, will you? Another minute or two won't matter."

James Lee stopped and waited. His eyes measured the young Irishman. They were about the same height and size, slender heavyweights. Danny was fuller around the shoulders. Powerful wrists and hands projected from the sleeves of his shirt. A person would think twice before getting into a fight with O'Halloran. They faced each other in almost the same spot in which, fifteen minutes earlier, Frank DaVini had yelled, "Jesus Christ!", pointing at three-six-eight and demanding, "What the hell is this?"

"This is a fine time to be coming in, Cooley."

"I had something to do. Sorry."

Immediately James Lee wished he had not added the last word, for Danny pounced on it. "Sorry! My God! You drag in here at nine o'clock and all you can say is you're sorry."

James Lee shrugged. "That's what I said. What do you want me to do, crawl in here on my hands and knees? I told you I had something to do."

"This is a job, Cooley, you know."

"I know this is a job, O'Halloran. What did you think I thought it was?" He was thinking that O'Halloran reminded him of Captain Queens in Louisiana who had yelled at him, "This is the army, Cooley, y'know." He had had to swallow a lot in the army, but things were different now.

"This is a business to make money. Everybody

loses when you keep a car laid up here this long. There were three extras around here but I saved the car for you."

James Lee knew this was not true. O'Halloran already had the reputation of not doing anybody any favors unless he was paid for it. He said nothing. He was aware of the mechanics peeping over the railing upstairs. He felt hot and uncomfortable around the neck.

"Some of you guys give us a hard time, dragging in here at all hours."

"Some of *what* guys?" James Lee demanded. Did he mean the Negro drivers, or hackies in general?

"Some of you friggin' drivers," said Danny, who had not meant that at all. He turned on his heels and walked toward the steps he had just come down. "If you want this job you had better start acting like it." And, like Frank DaVini, he added: "Put some money on that clock."

James Lee got into the cab and drove it out of the garage. He thought back over the conversation to see if he had held his own. He always did badly in these examinations. Part of the price of being a Negro was that he was never satisfied with the fight he put up for his dignity and pride. He decided he had not said anything wrong but that he had not said enough. He should not have let Danny have the last word. He was a hackman with a good record. He could get a job anywhere.

Upstairs, Danny O'Halloran settled down onto his favorite stool near the grease pit. "One of these days," he said, "I'm going to kick that nigger where it will do him the most good."

The three mechanics agreed that they would like to see Danny try. It happened that all of them were small men and this fact spiced their resentment of Danny, who towered above them like a golden-haired Hollywood hero. They would like to see him in a scrap with somebody his own size, though they were not certain they would want James Lee, a Negro, to win.

One of them winked at the others and said to Danny: "So go ahead, kid. You had just got your hand on her brassiere and she had said, 'Please don't, Danny darling . . .' "

The young dispatcher ignored the sarcasm. "Oh, yes . . ." He closed his eyes and let his mind swim in the gruesome details.

There was a fan in the telephone booth where James Lee was, but he was hot. He had just come from the room in which he had expected to find Essie waiting for him.

"Hello, Iretha. This is James Lee."

"Hello, James Lee," said Iretha, as if they were old friends.

James Lee had met her only once and he had not liked her. It had been a dinner for three couples, a quiet, pretentious affair that nobody enjoyed. He had known what Iretha was thinking when she looked at him: that he was strictly no account and was taking advantage of her poor little sister.

"Is Essie Dee there?"

"Yes, uh-huh, she's here."

"Can I talk to her?"

"Just a minute." Iretha almost sang the words. James Lee hated her cooing voice. It was sweet and nasty, like syrup that clung to your fingers. It was typical of that phony crowd Iretha ran around with. Why did Essie have to run up there everytime she and James Lee had a fight? She had said she hated Iretha's way of life, yet as soon as something went wrong they became thick as peas in a pod.

"Hello, James Lee." It was Iretha's oozing voice again.

"Yes, Iretha?"

"I'm sorry, but Essie says she doesn't want to talk with you."

"But . . ."

"I'm sorry, James Lee."

Iretha had hung up the receiver. James Lee's lungs were empty. He wanted to hit somebody. He cursed into the dead phone and slammed the mouthpiece onto its cradle. He had passed three fares rushing back uptown to see Essie and now he did not have a penny on the clock. He cursed again and rushed outdoors to his cab.

8

Morning on Lenox Avenue was like a blue song, soft and soothing, with a steady bass beat, unhurried, going nowhere. The doors of the saloons, the shoe shops, and the fish-and-chip joints were thrown open, but it was too early for customers. One by one the corner bums took up their stations, the old folks brought their folding chairs out to the sidewalk or found seats near the open windows of stuffy apartments, and the blue song of Harlem wandered on.

"Hey, man," called Timmy, who was known as the Creep, "Whatcha know, John Lewis?"

"Man, I don't know nothing," said John Lewis as he shook hands with Timmy. When John Lewis took his hand away he had a dollar bill hidden in his palm that he put into his already bulging pocket.

"Let that roll on one-six-three," said Timmy, "and I'll be collecting from you at about five P.M."

"You've got it working, Pops."

John Lewis continued his morning stroll down Lenox Avenue. Beyond the door of Mabel's Beauty Salon was Mabel herself. She was plump, forty, and cheerful, with deep dimples and an extraordinary head of long, blue-black hair.

"Hey, John Lewis, you big black handsome thing, you."

"Hey, baby, you sweet little bundle of female, you."

Mabel left her customer and went to the cash register. She took out five one-dollar bills that she gave to John Lewis.

"I'm playing single action, John, honey. I want a four to lead."

"You got it coming, baby, you got it coming."

On down Lenox Avenue walked John Lewis.

"Hey, John Lewis, what you like today?"

"Everything, man. I like everything."

"Put my money on two-twelve."

"You got it coming."

Farther.

"Hey, John Lewis, sweet poppa."

"Hey, baby, you look good enough to eat."

"Take my money, you robber. I'm still playing six-nineteen, and it's beating me to death."

"It's coming, baby. Just hold on."

"John Lewis, you people must have those numbers fixed. You see how I missed those figures Saturday? I came so close I got a good mind never to play no more."

"Well, you know what Suzy Ann told Nappy Chin?"

"No. What?"

"She says, 'If you keep on gambling, you're bound to win.'"

"John Lewis, you're crazy. Here, put this on my regular figure."

"You got it coming," said John Lewis. "You got it coming."

The most popular gambling game in New York City, and especially in Harlem, is the numbers. The poorest, most miserable creature alive can play. To try his luck, all he needs is a penny, and if his guess is right the numbers bank will pay him six dollars in return. The odds against his winning are a thousand to one, and his payoff is only six hundred to one, but this disparity is somewhat compensated for by the comparative ease with which he can play this supposedly illegal game. The fat lady upstairs who sits at home all day with her cats and dogs, the grasping little man in the candy store across the street, the furtive, over-dressed loafer with glistening shoes who is standing on the corner at sunrise—each will take a bet on the numbers. The penny bet is the stock in trade of a multimillion-dollar business with its headquarters downtown in the city's financial district. This business is incorporated, after a fashion; it has its stockholders, its officers, its workers, and its payroll. Its volume of business is steady, and it is seldom in crisis, for it is based on that most solid and persistent of all American phenomena—the dream.

John Lewis was a large brown man with a good-natured smile and a carefully cultivated mustache. He was extremely attentive to his long black hair, which was waved and set regularly in a local beauty salon patronized exclusively by men. His rich voice was warm and friendly and especially appealing to women. Men were uncomfortably aware of his masculinity, but they admired him. More important for his business, everybody trusted him. If your number hit, you never had to look for John Lewis. He would search you out and put every penny in your hand, no ifs, ands, or buts.

Before the war John Lewis had been a heavy-weight boxer down in Washington, D. C. Promising, the wily managers had said, a real comer, a good strong boy who can take a punch. One night he was knocked out in the second round of a preliminary bout in Uline Arena. He blinked up at the lights and the counting referee and concluded that there was a lot more to boxing than being able to take a punch. He said to himself: John Lewis, stop making a fool of yourself. You better cut out this nonsense before you get your head knocked off. After that he quit the ring for good.

During the war he had distinguished himself not only as a truck driver in Patton's Transportation Corps, serving in Africa and Italy, but also as a black marketeer. He sold everything from sweaters and shoes to jeeps, and once, in Rome, he managed to dispose of a six-ton truck. Consequently he had a few thousand dollars saved at the end of the war. He decided to settle in Harlem, telling himself that a big man like him needed a big place to live. John Lewis liked handsome women and fast living, and so his savings disappeared quickly. But he had learned how to get along in New York City. Writing the numbers came natural to him. He walked the streets like a native. He was a good fellow to swap drinks with at the Theresa Bar or the Palm Café where the entertainers and the sporting crowd gathered.

Six days a week he took his morning stroll down Lenox Avenue, turning into the numbered streets along the way. He had trained himself to carry all the bets in his head, and a curious policeman could search John Lewis all he wished, he would never find a slip of paper with numbers written on it. Sometimes when John Lewis did more business than usual he would go home two or three times so that he could write the numbers down there.

By ten-thirty John Lewis had finished his pickups and was in his apartment where he and his wife Ada totaled the day's receipts. There, until early afternoon when the first race was run, people came in to place bets with him. At one-fifteen the pickup man came from the numbers bank and collected the money and the receipts. After the third race was run, if there had been any hits, the pickup man came again and paid John Lewis, who in turn paid the lucky player.

It was a good living for him. He carried a large book of regular players. He was certain of seventy dollars a week, and with his cut from winnings he often earned a hundred. There was really no risk involved. The big banker took care of any difficulty with the police, and John Lewis had no fear of losing any money because as the middleman he never risked any.

This morning as soon as John Lewis got home he sat down at a table and began writing down the numbers that had been bet with him on the street. Ada came out of the bedroom and spoke with her lips close to his ear.

"How's it coming?"

He shivered. This always happened when she petted him. It was silly. He could never understand how such a little woman could have so much power over a big man like him.

"Come on, baby," he said, "don't start your funny business. Let me write this down."

When he had first come to New York he had sported with the tall yellow glamour girls. It had seemed that a big man like him needed a shapely, statuesque woman to set him off well when he appeared in public. Ada had changed all that the day he walked into Don's Bar-B-Que where she waited table. At first he had resisted the idea—"Why, she's only as big as a minute," he told himself—but six weeks later they were married.

Now she was wearing a black mandarin costume and Chinese bangs. The hair at her neck was caught with a bright red ribbon that matched the color of her lips. She sat on his knee and rested an elbow on his shoulder. She touched her lips to his forehead.

"Nora just called," Ada said in a voice that seldom went above a whisper. "She wants to know if we're going over to Atlantic City this week end."

John Lewis jotted down the last of the figures. "Baby, to tell you the truth, I don't know. Maybe I'd better stick close and see how everything works out before we start spending money."

She kissed his neck below the ear. "Is it going all right?"

"It'll work out, I think." John Lewis rubbed his chin with his hand. "I've got to play my cards close and I need a little luck."

This was absolutely true. Two weeks before, John Lewis had forsaken the relative security of the ordinary numbers writer. He had reasoned that a man could not stop growing. A big man had to step out and take a chance. Months ago he had sat down and taken stock of his progress. He and Ada had a few hundred dollars in the bank and he had just had a run of luck with the ponies at Saratoga. Why not make some real money for himself and step into the big league? Instead of just writing the figures and turning the profits over to someone else, why not *bank* them himself? He knew the numbers game and he had good contacts. If he nursed his little stake along he might build it into a real fortune. Others had done it.

He knew very well that you did not rush headlong into establishing a numbers bank. Harlem, like all of New York, was divided into carefully guarded sections, and each section had been allotted long ago to specific groups. The overall system was controlled by men with enough power to stay on top and dictate which groups operated and which did not. A new bank, even a small one of a few hundred dollars, could succeed only at the expense of another bank, so you had to have permission to operate. You had to pay off the right people and you had to have luck. If you opened a bank without permission, you very quickly ran out of luck. Many an upstart numbers entrepreneur had ended up dead.

But so far John Lewis had been smart. He had used his good contacts and had played them right so that the big boys had finally given him a nod. To be sure, it was not much of a nod. They had just made a little corner for him. They wouldn't help him, and he had to pay them to operate. But they wouldn't bother him. In a few months, with luck, he would be in the Cadillac class.

He had set up operations with two thousand dollars. Twelve playing days had now passed and his bank had grown to thirty-one hundred dollars.

Hubert could never relax until he had played his number. Whatever amount of money he had in his pocket urged him on toward his goal, the numbers writer. Until the bet was safely placed, he felt he was playing a foolish and dangerous game by carrying the money in his pocket. So he never tarried. As he rushed along the sidewalk, if anybody spoke to him he would give a hasty answer and continue on his way.

"Hey there, Mister Hubert," called Mrs. Jonas, the old woman who sold sweet-flavored crushed ice from her little cart on One hundred and twenty-sixth Street. "What you liking today?"

"I reckon a four," said Hubert and hurried on. Mrs. Jonas made a mental note of the four. All morning she would be asking passers-by what they liked. When she had decided which digit was the most impressive she would risk a quarter on it, hoping for a two-dollar return. This form of betting was called the single action, where instead of trying to catch three numbers you tried for one.

The fellows who stood in front of the Crystal Bar had Hubert marked down as a character who was always good for a laugh. They had learned from John Lewis that Hubert played large sums of money on the numbers and this convinced them that he was crazy. The numbers he played sounded weird to them, and, worse, he kept changing them all the time. This was something no good player was supposed to do. So each day when they saw him approach they would nudge each other and greet him with exaggerated respect.

"Good morning, Mister Hubert," they chorused, bowing at the waist.

"Good morning." Hubert's response was always brisk and unfriendly. Negroes who stood on the corners laughing loudly and drinking wine were the very ones who kept the race from advancing.

Flash was a kind of leader of the group because he was very resourceful in finding ways of obtaining sneaky pete, the local term for cheap sherry and muscatel. This morning he removed his hat and smiled broadly, showing several gold teeth that had been installed in better times. "May I ask what number you're playing today, Mister Hubert?"

"Four-seventeen," said Hubert. He always told them, although he knew they were laughing at him. It gave him pleasure to think that when his number came they would remember having heard it that morning.

They were sure that 417 was not a good number because fours and sevens had played the week before. So they had a good laugh wondering how much money Hubert was throwing away again. Flash remembered he had an aunt who lived at 417 St. Nicholas Avenue, but this disturbed him only a moment. He and his aunt were not on good terms—she had refused to have anything more to do with him until he found a job—and it was not likely that her address would indicate a lucky number.

Hubert spoke abruptly. "John Lewis, how much money do you get for a seven-dollar hit?"

"I don't know right off, Mister Hubert."

"Well, figure it up then," said Hubert impatiently.

After a minute John Lewis said, "That comes to four thousand two hundred dollars."

Hubert thought about it. Forty-two hundred dollars was a very satisfactory figure. He held the seven dollars toward John Lewis.

"Put that on four-seventeen. Four, one, seven."

John Lewis took the money. "Boy, you're really playing them heavy."

"That's the only way I know how to play 'em."

"Well, good luck to you." John Lewis put the money in his pocket. Hubert went out, and Ada closed the door after him.

"That poor little man," said Ada. "Just throwing away good money after bad. Don't you feel sorry for him?"

"If I started feeling sorry for people, I'd have to go into another business. The reason I will make it in this town is because I save all my sympathy for myself. And you, of course."

"But you know he doesn't have a chance, the way those fours and sevens were running last week."

John Lewis put his big hands on her waist and lifted her into the air. "Baby, remember that every number is a good number until it *don't* come out. Fellow was telling me just the other day about a time back in the depression when two led off every day for sixteen straight days. What do you think of that?"

He set her down and went back to the card table where he continued his figuring. Strictly speaking, it was true that yesterday's number might come back today, but it was highly unlikely. But why should he care if Hubert threw his money away? How could he make a living if there were no fools with money? He turned his mind away from the little man and the bad bet. The question was: How much money could he back with his own bank and how much would he have to pass on?

9

Noon eased itself into the Manhattan streets. The sun hung high over Harlem, and its heat was heavy as a white cloak over the flat roofs and the gray streets. Children sought the coolness of dark basements and dank hallways. The old people sat near their windows and looked with indifference out onto the shimmering streets. Behind the lunch counters brown girls and yellow girls, irritated by the heat and their own perspiration, grouchily served up frankfurters with sauerkraut, hot sausages with mustard and relish and onion, milk shakes, malteds, coffee, and orange juice; served these to impatient clerks and laborers and helpers' helpers, to shoppers, policemen, and hack drivers. Preachers napped and dreamed of churches larger than the Abyssinian. Lawyers and petty real-estate brokers planned and schemed and gamblers figured. A con man dropped a wallet with a hundred-dollar bill in it to the sidewalk in front of the Corn Exchange Bank and waited for a sucker to fall for the age-old game. A hustler sat in her apartment on Sugar Hill sipping cocktails with a white merchant from downtown who was taking a long week end, sized him up, estimated his worth. Madam Lawson shuffled her cards, Madam Fatima stared into her silver crystal ball, and turbaned Abdul Ben Said of the ebony skin mumbled an incantation to the black gods of old, and lo! all of them saw glory in the morning if not sooner. There, near the top of Manhattan Island, Harlem sizzled and baked and groaned and rekindled its dream under the midday sun.

As Hubert walked along One hundred and twenty-fifth Street, he was, after his own fashion, praying to God. These were hot, turbulent encounters accompanied by furious sounds and colors. The ordinary hum of the city, the horns and the whistles, the murmur of voices, the hoarse breathing of car and truck engines—all these city noises changed to shrill shrieks and senseless tumult when Hubert had a go at God. When he was a boy he had believed in the God of the Southern Baptist Church, the know-it-all dispenser of justice and glory at the end of a Christian life of trial and tribulation, showing off miracles and casting fallen sinners into the hellfire. Hubert had not really lived with God then—had just taken His existence for granted without really acknowledging it. But now he knew that God really did exist and that He was strictly responsible for everything, good or bad, and whenever He did not straighten up and fly right, Hubert gave Him down the country. Today as Hubert walked along he sometimes gestured violently to emphasize a point he was making. He paid no attention to the people who stared at him.

The tires of the car screeched to a halt. The driver pushed his head through the window and said lazily, "Hey, Pop, wassa matter? Got the blues? Tired of living, huh?" Hubert did not hear him. He stepped onto the curb and continued on his way.

"God, You may be all-powerful, but as far as I am concerned You have been lax on the job. There's right to be done and You ain't doing it.

I have worked and tried and been beaten only to get up again. I never asked You for too much, either. What's a grocery store, a shoe repair shop, a little luncheonette? Now, I don't understand You. You know I deserve it, but You ain't helping me to get it."

Hubert bumped into a girl who said, "Damn, Mister, what you trying to do? Knock me down?" She cut her eyes at him and passed on.

Hubert stopped in front of Blumstein's Department Store and startled people nearby when he suddenly threw up his arm and pointed toward the many stories of concrete and brick that imposed themselves over One hundred and twenty-fifth Street. Hubert's lips were moving, but no sound came from them.

"Did I ever ask You for a store like Blumstein's? No, 'cause I know that ain't reasonable. Blumstein's was here before I got to Harlem and will be here when I'm gone. I don't begrudge them the money I paid them for that refrigerator back at the beginning of the war, or the rug that Gertrude wanted, or the two lamps, or any of those things we bought from them in the last twenty years." He waved his hand toward Woolworth's five-and-dime store next door to Blumstein's. Nor did he begrudge Woolworth the nickels and dimes he had spent there during the same period. He had heard it said that buying and selling were the life's blood of the nation. He believed in law and order—he had taken no part in either one of the two Harlem riots where people broke windows and looted stores. He believed in the system and that Woolworth and Blumstein had a right to keep their places in it.

"But what about my place?" he cried aloud, and again people stared at him. He wanted passionately to buy and sell, to be a man of commerce, even in the smallest sense. "Dammit!" yelled Hubert, "I deserve something."

A mounted policeman in front of Loew's movie house looked at Hubert uneasily but decided the little man was not worth the trouble it would take to dismount. Besides, he had quieted down now and was walking on.

Maybe You're punishing me for what happened between me and Gertrude, Hubert thought, but You know that ain't fair. If it wasn't for her I would've been out of Harlem long ago. In those days I wanted to take her with me. But she's the one that was responsible for me taking this job up here in Harlem and having to clean up after these no-account Negroes. I always could save money when I worked downtown, but once a man starts working up here he's lost. Another thing, God. I ain't never lost faith in You the way some folks have. You've got to exist or ain't nothing right.

Hubert walked on. "You owe me some luck, God. You owe me some luck."

Each time he saw Sister Clarisse he told himself: Lord, Lord, one of these days I'm gonna grab this little woman and I won't be able to let her go. That was the way he felt when he saw her face with its soft brown eyes and modest smile, the full yet young bosom panting under her lace blouse. Here was a woman! Half-forgotten urges welled up in him. He deserved a woman like this, he needed her, he would have her.

"I do declare now," said Sister Clarisse, "isn't this a nice surprise?"

Her twenty years in Harlem had in no way affected her soft Southern speech, and her voice created pictures in Hubert's mind. It was evening down home. Sister Clarisse, wearing a blue flowered dress, sat in a swing on the front porch. In her hand was a fan. Nearby, a pitcher of cold lemonade stood ready with two glasses. Hubert, a young man, had come courting.

"I hope you haven't had your lunch yet, because I've just been making some salmon salad I think you'll like." She indicated a chair for him and took a seat in the corner of the sofa. "Well, if you aren't the last person in the world I expected to see."

This was not exactly true, inasmuch as Hubert

had of late become a regular caller, but it pleased Sister Clarisse to pretend she was surprised each time he came.

She walked around the screen into her neat little kitchenette. "Well, if we're going to have lunch, I'd better get it fixed. Did you ever see so much hot weather in your life? I declare, if it gets any warmer I'll just melt, that's all."

He did not answer. She was becoming used to his long silences and she went on talking. She had heard it said at Little Calvary that Hubert was "peculiar in the head," but this did not disturb her. After all, she was not married to him, and he always behaved himself while he was with her.

Later, after they had eaten and she had served Hubert a glass of cold beer, he spoke abruptly. "Sister Clarisse, what do you think of me?"

"Well, now—"

"Do you like me?"

"Why, yes, of course—"

"Then listen," he said, and he went on to tell her about his dream. As he talked he held her with his eyes. She felt uncomfortable. Why in the world was he being so serious?

" 'Where'd you get the money,' you kept saying over and over again," said Hubert. "And you and me, we were on our way to San Francisco . . . together."

She did not know what to say about such a

dream. She shifted her weight on the couch and said nothing. Unaccountably, she crossed her legs.

"I want you to know I think an awful lot of you, Sister Clarisse," said Hubert.

She began to move her fan furiously. Leftright-leftrightleftrightleftright. "Well, I'm glad, Mister Hubert."

"I'm not happy at home, and I ain't been for a long time."

"Now, Mister Hubert, I don't think you should be telling me such personal things—"

"Hush now, Sister Clarisse. I want you to listen because I'm building up to something I want to say." Her fan took up a calmer rhythm as Hubert settled in his chair. He went on: "I been watching you and thinking about you and I've figured out that, like me, you must be awful lonely, too—"

"Mister Hubert, please—"

"It's the truth, ain't it?"

She hesitated. The fan slowed. Left . . . right . . . left . . . right. "Well," she said, "naturally, we all get lonely sometimes, especially somebody who is all by herself." Left . . . right . . . left . . . right . . .

"Well, now, I know you never gave me no call to talk like this, but wouldn't you rather me speak what's on my mind than hide it?"

"Well, yes," she said, "I expect I would."

This was not true either. She was a woman

who liked pleasant banter, but when the conversation took a serious turn she quickly lost interest, or, if it was pointed at her, she became warm and embarrassed, as she was now. She could not help noticing his eyes. They were definitely not ordinary. Remembering what they whispered about Hubert at Little Calvary, she began to wonder if she had been wise in encouraging his attention. She did not mind a casual flirtation but . . . left right left right left . . . What was he saying?

". . . out in California. They say a man with a little shop can live real comfortable there. Lots of people go out there when they're getting up in age because of the sunshine and all. Any day now, Sister Clarisse, I'm expecting to get the money and make this big move. When it comes—and it will come, it will come—I'll be asking you to come and go with me."

Her fan stopped abruptly. Only now did she understand fully what he was talking about. "Mister Hubert!" was all she could say, but the exclamation sounded ineffectual, without the outrage she wanted it to have. So she added, "Well, I never!"

"Well, now I said it," said Hubert, "and I'd be pleased if you'd think about it. I know it don't become a married man talking like this, but you know I ain't asking you to do no wrong. We're both lonely and we could make each other happy. If things work out right, would you—you know you ought to, but would you—come away with me?"

Sister Clarisse did not know what to say. She was frightened and very warm. Left right left right left right. Somehow Hubert had moved over to the couch and had her hand in his. She wanted to take it away, to smile, to say something, anything to regain control of the situation. Could Hubert be dangerous? He was acting peculiar, talking fantastically about impossible things, and here she was, alone with him.

"Brother Hubert," she began, "I do think I may have given you the wrong impress—" She became aware of a man's unfamiliar breath. His lips touched hers and she inhaled sharply. He stood up.

"I'll be going now," he said, "and please think about what I've said." He left.

Now she was really angry. Who did this man think he was? She would have to get him told, really put him in his place. But he was gone. She raised her fingers to her lips.

10

James Lee drew up to a corner where a red light was already holding a Checker cab. The driver was a Negro, and as a rule James Lee would have spoken to him. But halfway down the next block on the right-hand side of the street a lady was standing with a bag. She was almost certainly waiting for a taxi, and since both cars were empty they would have to race for her. So they pretended not to notice each other and waited for the light to change. The driver of the Checker was next to the curb and by an unwritten law the passenger belonged to him. James Lee could see that he was planning to jump the light as soon as it was safe to cross the intersection. James Lee had the same idea and a faster car. The light changed. James Lee jerked his foot off the clutch and simultaneously slammed the accelerator to the floor. The DeSoto leaped across the intersection. James Lee cut in front of the Checker, who gave a scream with his horn, and brought the DeSoto to a halt in front of the lady with the suitcase. She opened the door and got in.

"Boy, you sure must be hungry." The Checker had drawn up to the left of James Lee and the driver was yelling in an angry voice.

James Lee felt the blood rush to his head. "Aw, go get yourself a car and stop crying," he yelled.

The Checker driver was a middle-aged, stocky, brown-skinned man with rimless eyeglasses. "Some people will put their heads in a toilet for a buck," he said. He put the Checker in gear and drove away.

"Take me up to Seventy-third and Madison, driver. I'm in a hurry." She was a thin white woman with black hair and a voice that was cold and sharp. She was not the kind to take notice of two colored hackies who shouted at each other and almost wrecked their cars trying to get her as a fare.

James Lee eased the car into the traffic and headed uptown. He did not like having to beat another Negro out of a fare, and he wished he could explain to the driver that he really needed every nickel he could get that day to keep up his average. But why should he feel bad? It was dog eat dog out on the streets, and he had never noticed anybody holding back to let him get ahead.

"I do wish you would hurry, driver. I have a one-thirty appointment."

"I'm going as fast as the traffic will allow, Madam."

"Well, do the best you can."

He wanted to say something else, but the thought that he might knock himself out of a tip stopped him. Then he examined her face in his mirror. No, he decided, dried-up prigs like that would never tip more than a dime, not even if it were raining and you carried their suitcases for them. A dime was all they thought you deserved.

"I'm free as a bird," called Essie. Her voice sounded as if it belonged to someone else as it rang through the empty apartment.

"Do you hear what I say?" she demanded of the innocent walls and chairs and tables. "I'm free as a bird."

Yes, that black man had had her number, all

right, but he could forget it now. She had danced to his tune long enough. From here on in, the men would jump when she said jump and no one would ever push her around again.

Essie snapped on the radio and found a colored station. A tenor sax man was carrying the melody on a jump tune. She danced around the living room, enjoying the music even more because she knew her sister disapproved of these stations. She said their music was too loud and only backward Negroes listened to them. But today Essie was playing a game. This was her apartment and she could listen to any station she wanted. She closed her eyes and she was dancing with Javan Washington down in Cheraw, North Carolina. Javan had been sweet on her. Once he had taken her to a dance contest and they had won second prize.

The tenor sax moaned as the tune ran out. The announcer spoke of how much nicer life was for girls with lighter, brighter complexions. A girl who used Black & White Bleaching Cream was certain to get the man of her dreams. Essie sat on the window seat and looked out over the Hudson River to the New Jersey coastline.

Free? What did she mean? It was easier to say than to know. Her mind grappled with the definition.

When she had first come to New York and lived with Iretha and Hugh she had been uncomfortable among them and their friends. Even though it had been exciting to meet the important people who came to the house, she knew nothing of the things they talked about and she spoke very little for fear of saying something wrong. Who was she but a poor little Southern girl whose mother still took in washing down home? Who was she to be sitting among these doctors and lawyers and these fancy women with their beautiful clothes? Essie wanted to get out on her own. "Stay with us," Iretha had said. "Go to school and take one of those business courses. With your looks you'll get a good job in no time. And don't worry about money. Hugh and I aren't rich but we're doing all right. Stay with us, girl. Besides, it won't look right, your being my sister and working in somebody else's kitchen."

It had been a real struggle getting away from Iretha and Hugh. They had done so much for her that she had felt guilty leaving them when they were obviously sincere about wanting her to stay. Still, she knew she could not live with Iretha and Hugh. True, a sleep-in job was not much, but at least she had been on her own and free.

But not from loneliness. Then James Lee had made her days in the city complete and satisfying. During the hot months she especially liked to go to the beach with him. She loved his body, and when they played in the water she fancied she knew what was going on in the minds of the other women. And, if she said so herself, she was not bad looking. She belonged with him. On Thursday nights and the few week ends when she could come to the city they went to movies and parties and danced at the Savoy.

Sex with him had come about naturally. Their first night together had been good, complete and satisfying. Now sometimes she had thoughts that were frightening because of their strange and forbidden depths. In her sex experience she had unlocked a new and secret part of herself more wonderful than all her girlish dreams had ever imagined.

"I love you, James Lee."

"Do you, Essie?"

"I love you, I love you. There's a song that goes like that."

"Say it over again."

"I love you."

Their murmurings in the night had been strangely real. She had felt as if she had no skin, as if every nerve were tingling, every part of her alive and sensitive to his fingers and lips.

Essie trembled and closed her eyes. Despite all this happiness she could now feel that she was freeing herself. Where had it all started? She had to be able to put her finger on it and explain it to herself. She had to be certain.

The Sunday they went to Central Park was a fine, bright day, the first warm Sunday that spring. She had asked him to bring her because she had never been rowing before. She was wearing a brightly colored sailor's outfit, and James Lee teased her, saying he thought she was over-doing it for a mere rowboat. But she could tell he liked the way she looked.

He rowed well and easily, moving from one part of the lake to the other with little effort. His strokes were rhythmical, one oar biting the water at a time so that the boat moved along smoothly. She complimented him. She knew he was show-ing off a little, but that was nice, too. It was a peaceful day, and she was glad they had come. Then she thought that she would like to row.

"But why? Aren't you comfortable?"

"I just want to try. Please, James Lee."

"Aw, come on and relax," he said. "These oars are heavy."

She was vaguely disappointed. Why didn't he want her to try?

"Please, James Lee."

"Okay," he sighed. "Come on."

He frowned as he helped her into the stern seat and took hers in the bow. He would not smile when she winked at him. Like a boy, she thought, whose toys have been taken away. Well, she would not ask him anything. She would learn to row all by herself.

But he was right. The oars were heavy. She had hardly begun before one of them slipped through the oarlock into the water. She managed to retrieve it, but not before she had dropped the other, which he lifted from the water and passed to her without saying a word. In a few moments she was exhausted and frustrated with her inability to make the oars move with any sort of rhythm. She gave them up and went back to her seat, and did not say a word the rest of the time they were on the lake. For days she was angry with him—a quiet, frustrating anger because it puzzled her. They had bitter little quarrels over trifles. Then gradually she had stopped thinking about the lake, but she had never forgotten it.

Essie went to the radio, switched it off, and returned to the window seat. A tug with yellow lettering on it chugged down the Hudson, leaving a pencil of black smoke.

Only now, as she looked back, was Essie aware that she had attached so much significance to that little incident. Since that day there had been a new thing between her and James Lee. Figuratively she had tried many times to row the boat and he had prevented her.

The abortion. What had a rowboat to do with that? She shut her eyes tight. It hurt almost physically when she thought of it. They were connected, the rowboat and the abortion, both parts of a large pattern. She had given in to him on that most important of things, their baby.

"Don't you see, Essie," he had said, "that's the ugly way to get married? We'd always feel we'd been forced into it."

"But if we love each other . . ." She had paused, afraid of the thought that had come to her. "You do love me and want to marry me, don't you, James Lee?"

"You know I do, baby, but not this way. As soon as we're ready we'll get married and have a great big family. But let's not start out this way."

It had all been wrong. The reasoning had been twisted out of shape, but she had listened and been persuaded. Even now the memory of what they had done made her go cold all over, trembling because it was like yesterday, the abortion, and there was nothing anybody could do about it.

She opened her eyes. The tugboat with the yellow lettering disappeared around a bend of the river trailing its thin, black ribbon of smoke, and her thoughts rushed on.

11

He was confused. He did not want to lose Essie, but he did not want to marry her. That was what she had wanted all the time, that was the only thing that would really make her happy, and it was the one thing he was not willing to do. Why couldn't things ever stay as they were when they were going well? He was not in love with her. When you were "in love" with a woman you were carried away by her good looks, her way of doing things. Everything about her overpowered you and finally you gave in. That was being in love.

So he was not in love with Essie. He had been sleeping with her for more than a year and he felt he knew her like a book. She was that simple, and she was definitely not overpowering. She was just a pretty little girl from the South who was crazy about him.

But his life was stuck like a car in the mud. It was a lot of disconnected pieces and he could not make any sense out of them. He felt guilty about his treatment of Essie, and at the same time he knew he had nothing to feel guilty about. Women seemed born to hard luck. The trouble was that he was twenty-six years old and he did not feel he had hold of anything, that he was growing. Essie was about the only thing in his life that he was sure of, and he had the strange fear that if he lost her everything might fall apart.

The traffic was jammed for three blocks leading up to the pier. The "Queen Mary" gave a loud, anxious groan and waited. The traffic lurched forward a few feet and came to a sudden halt. The cab was a hot box, and James Lee's clothes were soaked with his sweat. His buttock itched, but he had two women passengers and could not give it the hard scratching it needed. He had to content himself with squirming in the seat, at the same time keeping an eye on his two passengers in the rear-view mirror to see if they were paying any attention to him.

He thought about his twenty-three months in the army. There were only three distinct things that ever came to mind: Leroy Butler, who stepped on a mine in Pyongyang and was blown to bits; the grenade that exploded behind him while he was crawling and the sensation of a thousand needles stabbing at him; and a man he had known named McGowan.

James Lee had been looking at Leroy Butler just before the mine heaved up the earth with a crushing jar, and when everything had settled there was no trace of the man who had been there a few seconds before. At first he had not believed that he could have been looking at Leroy. Then, when he knew that Leroy really had been there, he had become filled with a horrified wonder. Why, you could be walking along and suddenly lose everything, absolutely everything, even form and substance. He had not known Leroy Butler very well and he had seen other men go down. But the idea of suddenly disappearing from the earth, leaving hardly a trace of your former existence, filled him with cold fascination.

It was natural, too, that he should remember the grenade. When it exploded he was crawling along near the rear of his platoon, almost un-afraid for a moment because they had just cleared

the rear area and could move ahead without fear
of snipers behind them. But the grenade had
come from behind. The explosion made everything seem ludicrous. When he remembered that
winter in Korea and the big push toward the
Yalu, it was neither the bitter cold nor even the
frozen corpses that came to mind. It was a question: How could an enemy have been behind
them when they had just cleared the area? It was
crazy, absurd, like everything else that bizarre
year.

He could not say why he thought of McGowan,
who was only one of the many characters he had
met. Besides, he had never liked the man. By all
rights he should have forgotten McGowan long
ago. . . .

He was a Negro on the same ward with James
Lee in the hospital near Yokohama. His bed was
in a corner and James Lee had the bed next to
him. He was squat and ugly and only shaved for
inspection. The few other Negroes in the ward
were ashamed of him and tended to avoid him
because of his blunt manner. James Lee probably
would have done the same, but during those first
few weeks he was unable to get out of bed. The
first time McGowan spoke to James Lee was on
the second morning during breakfast. He was sitting up in bed with the tray across his legs. He
had a habit of chewing and talking at the same
time.

"Boy, what are you doing over here?" There was not even a hint of friendliness in his gruff greeting. "You're a long way from home."

"I guess you are, too," said James Lee.

"Damn if I ain't," he agreed, and he laughed as if he had not considered that before. "They tell me you got your backside blasted. That right?"

"Yeah, that's right."

McGowan chuckled and went on with his breakfast. It had been only a few days since James Lee was wounded and he was in constant pain. He was sullen and angry. "I'm glad you can see something to laugh at, fella."

"Boy, if you can't see something funny in that you ain't got no sense of humor. Here you come all the way over here carrying that rifle and that other silly stuff they give you—all the way over here, just to get your butt busted open." He gave up the struggle to keep from laughing. His stunted little body shook so hard that he had to push his tray away to keep from knocking it over. "Man," he said, controlling himself for a moment, "you could've done that at home with less trouble."

James Lee watched in silence. The man was obviously crazy. He wished he could lift himself out of bed and get near enough to smash his fist into that open mouth with its uneven teeth.

McGowan finally stopped laughing, pulled his

tray back into position, and began piling his mouth full of food. "Where're you from, boy?"

"New York. Why?"

"New York," he grunted. "I thought they made some smart Negroes up there. Me, I'm just a Southern boy myself. Born and bred in Kentucky. Don't pay no attention to me 'cause I ain't got no sense."

"That," said James Lee dryly, "is one thing I can believe."

"What the hell were you doing over there in those hills, boy?" McGowan pointed in the general direction of Korea.

"They sent me over there," James Lee retorted. "What did you think?"

"The question is what did *you* think?" said Mc-Gowan. "You look halfway intelligent. Didn't you know you could get killed over there? Or did you think those Koreans and China boys were fooling?"

"Well, what were you doing over there?" James Lee assumed that everybody in the ward was a war casualty.

"Over where?" McGowan looked shocked, but his eyes twinkled. Again he pointed. "You mean over *there?* Boy, I wouldn't be caught dead or alive over there, not as long as they're shootin' and fightin' and fussin' and carryin' on." He winked at James Lee. "I got stomach troubles, man. They started just as soon as I heard where we were going and they ain't give me no rest since. My stomach bothers me all the time." He took a large bite of his food and chewed at it viciously. "You see, doctors don't know too much about the stomach."

"You mean there's nothing wrong with you?" James Lee said coldly. He had spent a lot of freezing nights in the mud of Korea and he had a few buddies who were still there. And then there had been Leroy Butler.

McGowan frowned. "Shhh, man. What you trying to do? Spoil my play?"

Later that same day he asked James Lee, "Say, man, do you know what these people are fighting about?"

James Lee said, "That's a silly question. How the hell would I know? Do you know?"

"No, I don't," McGowan laughed, "but I sure thought you did, coming in here with your butt full of lead and steel. And I'll tell you something else, Mister. If I ever go somewhere where they're shooting and killing, I'm gonna have a better reason than 'They sent me.' You can believe that."

James Lee grew to hate the man in the bed next to him. But he also became fascinated by him. Each morning he woke up with the thought: What is this fool going to say next? He learned that McGowan was from Louisville, Kentucky, and had spent a year in a Southern college before he was drafted. He was one of the few men on the ward who used the Red Cross library, but to James Lee he did not talk or act like an educated person. Nobody liked him, and for good reason. He was ill-mannered and aggressive. If the other men on the ward had a general joke, McGowan could see nothing funny about it. But when they showed movies in the ward McGowan always burst out laughing during the emotional scenes that were underlined with sentimental music, thereby embarrassing those who were involved in the picture's plot. The wonder was that nobody ever jumped him and gave him a good beating. Fights were not unknown on the ward, but everybody avoided McGowan and paid him a grudging respect with their unsuccessful attempts to ignore him.

One day he said to James Lee, "Man, you know what's wrong with you? You're in danger and you don't know it."

"What kind of danger, Professor?" James Lee had begun calling McGowan by the name the ward had given him.

"When that Chinese boy busted your backside with that grenade, didn't it make you stop and think? I'm not talking about being scared, but something else. Didn't you say to yourself, 'Why, I can get killed and won't have a damned thing to say about it'?"

James Lee had thought along those lines—or,

more accurately, he had felt along them—but he said nothing.

"Most people just go through life dancing to somebody else's tune," McGowan went on. "They get caught up early and they keep going along with the act just like sheep. And when they die it doesn't mean a damn thing because they never lived in the first place." McGowan put his head back on the pillow and stared up at the ceiling. "The first right is the right to live, boy. You got so many years and days and minutes to do something with your life. The only way you know what to do with your life is to think. Life is precious, man, and it makes me feel bad when I think of all those people who never had a life of their own because they let somebody else or some other thing have first call on it. It's like you're a house and you rent out all the rooms to other people and you end up sleeping outside because you didn't save any room for yourself. That's what it's like."

Lots of what McGowan said was too vague for James Lee to understand, but it almost always made him uncomfortable. He could seldom think of anything to say in reply.

One day McGowan suddenly asked, "Boy, you got a girl back home?"

"I got lots of 'em. Why?"

McGowan snorted, but James Lee felt he was on sure ground. It was true that he always had been popular with the girls and this was certainly something that little, ugly McGowan could not claim.

"I guess you trim 'em up a lot, don't you?"

"I guess I do 'trim 'em up' a lot, Professor," said James Lee with a sneer at the country expression.

"Boy, you sure are stupid," said McGowan.

James Lee's temper flared. "Have *you* got a girl?"

"Nope, but I got a wife," said McGowan, and already there was a snapshot in his hand that he passed to James Lee. The smiling woman was on the plump side but not unattractive. She held a baby in her arms. James Lee was surprised that she was not ugly. How in the world had she got stuck with a runt like McGowan?

"To really appreciate a woman, boy," McGowan was saying, "you've got to do more than trim her. You've got to get inside her soul and take a look at yourself. Then—and only then—you are cooking with gas." He took the snapshot and put it under his pillow. Then he lay back and closed his eyes and went to sleep.

The doctors were extremely attentive to McGowan. They were of the opinion that he had the only interesting case on the ward. He was constantly being fluoroscoped and X-rayed. Visiting specialists in internal medicine were always taken to McGowan's bed first. Regularly his stomach became upset and he was unable to hold anything on it.

"The secret," he said, "is concentration. I don't know why, but all I have to do is think I'm sick, and the next thing I know my stomach is acting up."

But one day McGowan's luck ran out. This was about five weeks after James Lee arrived. The chief of the medical service, Colonel Weylan, came in to see Private McGowan. He was to be congratulated, said the colonel. After exhaustive studies the medical staff had decided there was nothing wrong with Private McGowan that the rigors of infantry life could not cure. After a few more days of routine tests McGowan could re-join his old outfit. The colonel and the private shook hands. McGowan thanked the officer for the kind treatment he had received. The colonel left.

James Lee had his first good laugh in weeks. He himself had several more operations to undergo and no expectation of returning to the battle zone. It pleased him when he thought of McGowan being shot at in the continuous blizzard of a North Korean winter, and he suggested to the professor that he might even be killed—adding that no one deserved it more.

For his part, McGowan seemed to accept the tragic news with equanimity. He was happy, he said so that everybody could hear, to be leaving the hospital at last. He was an active man and did

not like sitting around in a robe and pajamas
with nothing to do. He promised to send them a
post card when he got to China.

It happened at three o'clock one morning. The
hospital was quiet and peaceful when McGowan
suddenly began to scream. They were blood-
curdling shrieks that shocked James Lee out of a
deep sleep. The lights began to go on. McGowan
was sitting up in his bed staring straight ahead as
if something on the other wall had pushed him
beyond the border of sanity. His shrill, horrified
cries made every man tremble. Sleepy-eyed
nurses, orderlies, and doctors came running. They
approached the frenzied, stunted little man cautiously. McGowan swung suddenly and viciously
and knocked one of the orderlies cold. The others
jumped him, but with surprising strength he
threw them off and jumped out of bed. With
agonizing screams he ran through the ward breaking windows and overturning tables. Suddenly he
stopped screaming and began to sing and dance.

> "'Cause my hair is curly,
> 'Cause my teeth are pearly . . .
> That's why they call me Shine." *

His pajama bottoms had fallen off now, and his
immobile face with its frenzied eyes made him
look like a crazy, wound-up doll. They rushed

* From "S-h-i-n-e." Words by Cecil Mack and Lew Brown.
Music by Ford Dabney. Copyright MCMXXIV and copyright
MCMXLVIII by Shapiro, Bernstein & Co., Inc., 1270 Sixth
Avenue, New York, N. Y.

him again. He fought them off, striking out
savagely at anyone who came near. James Lee sat
in his bed transfixed, certain this was a bad dream
that had suddenly erupted in his sleep.

The scene became as bizarre as a Halloween
party, as more orderlies arrived, equipped with a
strait jacket and sheets. They fell upon Mc-
Gowan as a mass, and he went down, still struggling and singing and kicking his feet as if to
dance. A doctor was standing near with a hypo-
dermic ready. When McGowan was safely fastened
inside the jacket the doctor approached and in-
jected the sedative. The muscles of McGowan's
face seemed to relax immediately, and he was
taken out of the ward. But as he was being
dragged through the door—and about this James
Lee was absolutely certain—McGowan turned his
head toward James Lee and winked.

"Driver!" The woman's sharp voice jerked him
out of his thoughts. "Driver!"

"Yes, Madam."

"Is this the quickest way we can go?"

"It's the quickest way I know," James Lee said.
"Midtown is always slow at—"

"Well, go over to Park Avenue. It seems to me
that Park Avenue ought to be quicker than Fifth."

Of course she was right. Park Avenue was always quicker than Fifth, but his mind had not
been on his work. When they reached the beauti-

ful six-laned avenue the traffic was moving slowly but steadily. James Lee glanced at his passengers in his mirror. The woman's husband was embarrassed because his wife had created a scene, but her look was one of sharp-faced triumph.

The one good thing about driving a cab, thought James Lee, is that when passengers get out of your car you will probably never see them again. He gassed his car into the Park Avenue overpass above Grand Central Station and thought of Essie again.

No, he did not want to marry Essie. But what did he want? What did he want of any woman? Damn! In four years he would be thirty. Time, they said, went faster after that. In almost no time he would be forty. His life was slipping away from him. He had to get himself in hand. The trouble was that a man's life ought to make some sense and it didn't, not his anyway. You spent all your time doing one thing or the other, and all you were really doing was trying to make life make sense. You never succeeded, he suspected, but you kept trying because there was nothing else to do. At twenty-six you ought to know something of what it was all about.

When his cab was empty again he drove to the West Side and pointed the car uptown. Perhaps he would go to Iretha's apartment and see Essie. It was better to settle these things before they became too involved.

12

It was one o'clock and John Lewis had a problem. He had sorted and checked all the bets he had received that morning. There was a lot of little money on some of the "hot" numbers and most of this he was passing on to the regular bank. All of the single-action money, the bets placed on a single digit, he was passing along because the odds against the player were cut down from a thousand to one to eight to one. He himself banked all the money that had been bet on odd numbers, those combinations of three numbers on which only one or two people were betting.

The problem concerned the money that had been played on the six possible combinations of seven, one, and four. Aside from Hubert's bet of seven dollars on 417, there were at least fifteen additional dollars bet on one of the other combinations of those three digits.

What puzzled John Lewis was that not one of the possible combinations was considered "hot." Most of the so-called hot numbers or lucky numbers changed from week to week. But some held on for months, and a few, like 711 and 510, have been considered hot for more than twenty years.

These lucky numbers were passed from block to block, and they reflected themselves in John Lewis's books. Two weeks before, 941 had played, and on the previous week either the four or the one had shown up in the numbers every day. So it was odd that anyone would consider a combination of the four, one, and seven lucky. Yet here were more than twenty dollars on those figures.

John Lewis separated this money from the rest on the table. He was no numbers player himself, for he knew there was no profit in it for anybody but the men behind the game. But without risking his money he sometimes tried to guess

how the number would run, and he was beginning to pride himself on having pretty good luck.
This morning he told himself that if he were a
player he would not bet a penny on any combination of four, one, seven. This was sure money for
the big banks. John Lewis made a sudden decision. He would keep this money himself and add
it to his bank. There was not one chance in fifty
thousand that a four or a one would show up that
day, and certainly not the whole number. It was
almost a certainty. He folded the bills, among
them Hubert's seven dollars, and pushed them
into his pocket. Now that he had made the
decision, he felt relieved. Why should he send
good money to the white man's bank? He went
to the kitchen and returned with a cold bottle of
beer. He imagined he could see the horses at the
starting gate in Saratoga. "Let 'em loose," said
John Lewis. "Let 'em run."

And so the great dream machine was wound
tight. The nickels were in the slots and the
players waited. Only a turn of the handle was
needed to set the whole thing in motion.

Oh, Lord, please let that number be 316 today. You know my life ain't been easy, me with
three mouths to feed and that man of mine done
snuck away like a dirty little coward. I done for-
give him, Lord, the way I know You wanted me

to—I never think no evil of him no more. But it's hard trying to feed these three kids on thirty dollars a week. Now, with a twenty-five-cent hit I could get shoes for little Johnny and Mary and Sarah Lou, and clothes to keep them in school. . . . So if You please, Lord, let that number come 316 . . .

A girl needs nice things or men just look the other way . . . dresses, slips, a handbag . . . Honest to goodness, I'm out of just about everything. Just can't seem to make enough to keep up. But if I can hit 212 today . . .

How a man can work so hard and never have any money I just don't know. If that 530 don't come today, I just don't know what I'm going to do. There's the television set to be paid, the refrigerator, the furniture and the car, all of which comes due the first of the month. Not to mention the rent that never stops and the gas and electricity and the telephone. I could take care of these things if 530 was to jump out just the way I played it. . . .

Let 728 come, and Harlem's gonna wake up and find out that I am here. I'll rent myself a suite up on the top floor of the Theresa and throw a party that will last a week. Then I'll buy myself the prettiest Cadillac Harlem ever saw.

It'll even have a television set in it. I might even send some money to Mama down home, too. She ain't been doing so good lately. . . .

Lord, I'm needing a new church so as I can help set these people back on the path of righteousness. I saw a nice big store at One hundred and thirty-sixth and Lenox, and I have made inquiries, and I know that store can be acquired for a hundred and twenty-five a month. Now, they want two months in advance, and You know I don't have that kind of money. It's the perfect site for the Blessed Lamb Holiness Church. From there, Lord, the truth of Your loving word will flow all over Harlem and bring these wayward sheep back to the fold. The number is 471, Lord, and I have played it in a six-way combination. Now, if in Your loving kindness You could see fit to make things go that way, O Lord, we would be eternally in Your debt as we are already. All these things we ask in Jesus' name.

Amen.

13

At two o'clock Mabel's Beauty Salon was working at full capacity. The three booths were occupied, and there were two women under the drying machines. The two operators who worked with Mabel paid her rent for the use of the facilities. There was a competition among the three as to who could do the fastest and the best work. Mabel was the oldest and, in a sense, the boss. She often complimented her two operators on their work, but the praise was always bestowed in a condescending manner, as if from the master to the student. Each one took great pains to point up the merit of her individual work. Each had her regular clients and each took great pride in sending them away fully satisfied. All things considered, they got on well together, for the shop was small and they had to make one another company for long hours six days a week.

Mabel was running a hot comb through a young woman's hair. "Girl, I swear it's getting longer and prettier every day."

"Oh, you think so, Miss Mabel?" The girl was pleased. Her mother was one of Mabel's customers and, no doubt, if she ever had a daughter she would be sent to Mabel's, too.

"I guess it's time you were thinking about getting married and making a family," said Mabel. She was intensely interested in the personal life of every one of her customers. This amounted almost to a passion, and a customer was hardly in the chair before Mabel, in her friendliest manner, began probing. Through the women who came to the shop Mabel managed to know what was going on in a large part of Harlem.

"Planning anything soon?" Mabel asked sweetly.

The girl smiled and blushed. Mabel laughed good-naturedly and dropped the subject. The girl's mother had an appointment for the next day, at which time Mabel would get the whole story.

Lucille was washing a client's hair. "What in the world did she do that for?" asked Lucille.

The running water muffled the woman's voice. "She said she was tired of living with him."

"At her age she won't get nobody else."

"I told her, but she said she don't want nobody else."

"Hmmm," said Lucille incredulously. "She ain't that old."

The third operator, Alice, called over. "What did he do, hit her or something?"

"No. She said he was running around with other women."

"Is that all?" Lucille clicked her tongue in disgust. "Well, what if he was? He's just a man. Everybody knows that a man is lower than a dog. He's just as good as the rest of them. She better hold on to him."

All the women in the shop voiced their agreement with Lucille. The voice of the announcer interrupted the swing music on the radio. "We have the first race in from Saratoga. Here are the results of the first race from Saratoga." Alice sat down beside the radio, where a pencil and a sheet of paper were waiting. She scribbled down the win, place, and show money as the announcer read them off. The music resumed.

Alice frowned when she had finished adding up the total.

She looked at Mabel and asked, "What did you play today, girl?"

"I just put five dollars on a four to lead," Mabel replied in her sweetest voice.

"Well, wouldn't you know it." Alice pushed the paper and pencil aside and went back to her customer. "As bad as I need money, and Mabel's hit that number again. There ain't no justice."

"Well, I play to win, girls," said Mabel. "Ain't no need in y'all getting mad at me."

Lucille said, "Don't tell me that number's a four when I have all my money on sixes."

"It's a four the way I figure it," Alice said.

Lucille left her customer and sat down in the same chair. "Here, girl, let me figure this thing out for myself." She began to count aloud. After a minute she said, "It's a four, all right." She crumpled the paper and threw it into the wastebasket. "Mabel, where in the world do you get such luck?"

Alice said, "That baldheaded old man of hers sure must be giving her some good treatment."

All the women laughed except Mabel, who smiled serenely.

"That I wouldn't deny," she said.

A pimp walking down Seventh Avenue looked down at the man who was shining shoes and said, "What's happening today, Pops?" And Pops looked up from the shoes and said, "Four times."

When the pimp got to One hundred and twenty-eighth Street a policeman was standing on the corner twirling his nightstick. "What's happening?" he asked the pimp, and the pimp replied, "A four's running."

The cop walked over to Lenox Avenue, where some young men were sitting in a car drinking beer. One of them said to the cop, "What's up, Doc?" The cop held up four fingers and walked on.

An old woman sitting in the shade of her newsstand called across the street, "What did he say?" The young men told her what the first number was.

The word went out from thousands of apartments and shops and stores. It crackled through the streets like electricity. People held up four fingers, whispered it out of windows, and tapped four times.

In a few apartments Negro girls examined long lists of three-number combinations from which they separated all those that had four in them. From these they separated all those that began with four. When they had the results, they presented them to their bosses, who got on the phone and began placing bets on the next two numbers with larger banks. This scene was duplicated thousands of times on the east and west sides of

Manhattan, in the Bronx and Brooklyn by white girls sitting at adding and calculating machines, and by their bosses who got on the phones and began placing what they called insurance money bets.

In a tall building downtown suave executives, the kind who first grow gray at the temples, and nervous executives, the chubby ones who sweat and chew cigars, checked with their accountants on the state of business, now that a four had played. The girls at the switchboards channeled the sudden flood that poured in at the same time six days a week. Here, at the summit of the business, men and women accepted these calls from district banks, then immediately sent the figures off to the accountants.

And in John Lewis's apartment he looked up from his pad and slapped his head with his hand. "A four! Well, what the hell do you know about that!" he said. "A four! Where did that come from?" He took his list and checked off his four money. There was no rush, no emergency. It was a routine matter. He smiled. Well, the suckers guessed *one* number right, anyway. He phoned in his insurance money but did not disturb the twenty dollars in his pocket.

14

"A black woman shall see hard times," Gertrude Cooley quoted to herself as she walked toward Lenox Avenue. A few minutes before, she had discovered her bureau drawer pried open and the seven dollars missing. It was possible that some-one might have sneaked into the apartment and stolen the money, but, as Hubert was missing, too, it was more than likely he had taken it. The gas and electric bills were long overdue and Consolidated Edison had already threatened to shut off the power. Gertrude did not know how she could get the money back even if she caught up with Hubert before he bet it, but she had to try. She walked in the general direction of John Lewis's house, hoping she would see him.

Mr. Curtis's candy store was empty except for the old man himelf. He was sitting behind the counter reading a newspaper with the help of his steel-rimmed glasses. The store was old and dusty, chock-full of penny candy, comic books, vending machines, notebooks, pencils, and a variety of useless gadgets for children. The few people who patronized the store came from force of habit. Mr. Curtis did not seem to care any more, so long as he kept a roof over his head and was his own boss.

"Mrs. Cooley, ain't seen you in I don't know when. Come on in here. How are you?" He was a short little man, a brown West Indian with a completely bald head. His lively eyes smiled and frowned as their owner's moods changed. "Mister Hubert? No, he ain't been in here since last week sometime." Then he swung to his favorite subject, politics and The Black Man. "Say, did you read this week's *Amsterdam?*" He held the paper up in the air and slapped it with the back of his hand. "The white man's up to the same old tricks. They appointed this fellow Clarkson to the

Interior department. You know him—his father owns all those funeral homes. Sent that boy to Harvard. He's supposed to be one of us but he wouldn't give a black man the time of day. He made an Uncle Tom statement about that boy they're trying to frame down there in Florida. But he's supposed to be in Washington representing us. Can you beat that!" He looked over his glasses at Gertrude and saw that she was not listening. "Are you all right, Mrs. Cooley? Something the matter with Mister Hubert?"

"No, nothing's the matter, Mr. Curtis." She walked to the door. "I'll be seeing you."

"If I can do anything to help, Mrs. Cooley," he said, "you just give a yell."

"Nothing's the matter," said Gertrude, "but thanks anyway."

Gertrude walked to Lenox Avenue. The afternoon was hot, but there were quite a few people on the street. Lord, Lord, thought Gertrude, where in the world am I supposed to start looking for that crazy man? Where did I sin to deserve all this misery? I must be about the unhappiest woman alive.

She had known Lenox Avenue for more than thirty years, but now she seemed to see it with new eyes, with deeper, more terrible understanding. Many of the faces were familiar: the young men on the corner laughing and boasting of empty accomplishments; old Slim Thomas who had drunk enough wine for the day and now lay asleep on the sidewalk near the Paradise Bar; the old men and women who sat on their folding chairs outside the stores and shops; the boy with the suit on the hanger stealing into Sol's pawnshop; the girl chewing gum behind the hot-dog stand on the corner; the insurance collectors and the furniture collectors and the salesmen with their bags full of sparkling junk and Bibles and cheap tapestries—all these familiar parts became a whole, complete picture as Gertrude looked at them, and the street with all its superficial color and sound became one flat, bluish gray, a dull, monotonous drone. Among these parts Gertrude saw herself, ungainly and ugly and tired in her work clothes. Most of us are just strivers, Gertrude thought, but strivers who never get anywhere. We just follow one day after another until the end comes, and, thank God, it comes soon. Gertrude knew, as she always had known, that you had to make the best of a bad situation. But today remembering the thirty years of her life spent near Lenox Avenue, years that seemed completely wasted, it was almost too much for her.

Suddenly she wanted to scream. She wanted to put her clenched fists to her head and yell bloody murder at the top of her voice. She wanted to break out of herself and make her voice heard everywhere. You couldn't just sit and take it forever. You had to cry for help. If you were being sucked under, if you were drowning, you screamed for somebody to throw you a lifeline.

She clenched her fists and opened her mouth to give way to that desperate need, but that was all. She was Gertrude Cooley who lived on One hundred and twenty-sixth Street, and everybody in her block knew her. When she walked down the street they said, "Good morning, Mrs. Cooley," and "How are you today, Mrs. Cooley?" They respected her, and women often came to her for advice because they knew she was one of the strong ones. She could not let herself go, not ever. She let her arms hang loose at her sides, and as she relaxed she began to tremble. She felt she had just had a narrow escape from something terrible and unknown.

She motioned to Flash, who was standing on the corner with his friends. He immediately detached himself and came over, removing his hat as he approached.

"Flash, is the first one out yet?"

"Yes, ma'am. It's a four."

"Thank you, Flash."

"Any time, Mrs. Cooley, any time."

She walked toward home. There was no use trying to find Hubert now. She would have to find another way to pay the gas and electric bill. Perhaps James Lee would have the money.

On One hundred and twenty-sixth Street Mrs. Jonas was scraping ice for two little girls who held their hands high so Mrs. Jonas could see their pennies. She put the ice in paper cups and flavored it with chocolate syrup. The girls squealed eagerly as they exchanged their money for the cups.

"I declare, Mrs. Cooley," Mrs. Jonas said, "you ain't looking so good today. What's the matter?"

Gertrude sighed. "A black woman born into this world shall see hard times."

"I know it's the truth," Mrs. Jonas said. She believed in all the old sayings. She sat on her folding chair and drew up the other one that she kept for company. "Come on, Mrs. Cooley, let's sit and chat a while."

But Gertrude did not feel like chatting. She excused herself and went into her apartment.

15

Actually, he had no business worrying about Essie, he told himself. She was only one woman, and he had plenty of opportunities to make time with other girls, especially the ones who had gone to school with him. When he happened to meet them on the street they usually made it plain that they would welcome a call from him. Very often when Essie was working in White Plains he took advantage of these opportunities. Then there were the women he met when he worked the night line. He wondered what Essie would think if she knew that there were many women who would rather sleep with him than pay their fares. They were not usually whores, either, but ordinary women, colored and white, often very well-to-do. They liked his looks. He wondered what Essie would say if she knew that the city was full of opportunities for a man like him. But why worry about Essie at all? She was just—

"Where're you going, driver? Isn't this the address I gave you?"

The passenger was a man who usually ordered people about. He and his companion wore cool summer business suits and an air of self-importance.

James Lee mumbled, "Sorry," stopped the car, and backed up to the entrance of the apartment building where a tall, gray-haired doorman touched the visor of his cap as he helped the passengers to the street. The fare was eighty cents and the man told James Lee to keep the change.

"Thanks."

"That's all right, George," said the man pleasantly. He walked into the apartment building with his companion and the doorman slammed the taxi door shut.

Late one Saturday night not many months before a white passenger had called James Lee

"George." James Lee had brought his car to a sudden halt, dragged the man out of the back seat, and knocked him to the sidewalk, where the man had apologized, explaining that he called everybody George, not just colored people. James Lee had driven away and left the man sitting there. He was often confused about what to do when he was called "son" or "boy," because an older white man might call anybody that. But he was never in doubt about George. This time, however, he had been caught completely unaware. The man had gone into the building and there was nothing he could do without feeling silly. He could not even show the minimum protest—to curse the passenger and throw the change in his face. A taxi drew up behind, forcing James Lee to drive away. Petty frustration gripped at him.

Then he knew what he had to do. He would go see Essie and have it out with her. This day everything had gone wrong for him, and it was all her fault because she was on his mind, bothering him. Nothing would be right until he settled with her. He pointed the car toward Harlem.

He had been to Iretha's apartment only once, and he had not liked it then. Now he disliked it even more, and he knew why. It was in one of those modern buildings at the foot of West One hundred and fifty-third Street. Negroes had only recently moved in, and there were still a few white families in the building. Most of the new occupants were big-shot professional people—doctors, lawyers, real-estate brokers, well-paid civil servants, and racketeers—that group of colored folks who always seemed to have everything going their way. When James Lee was around them he felt almost insignificant, just the way he did when rich white people got into his cab. That time Iretha had invited him and Essie to dinner—just to examine him, he was sure—he had felt clumsy and uncomfortable all evening.

"Oh, it's you," Essie said. She held the door open for him and told him to come in. She was calm and pretty. He was irritated that she had obviously not been crying. He remembered now that he had not had a bath or changed his clothes, and he needed a shave. The fancy apartment intimidated him, made him feel dirty. Who the hell did Essie think she was?

As they faced each other in the living room he began aggressively, "Look, baby, what is this business? I call you up on the telephone and you don't want to talk to me."

She shrugged. "I didn't want to talk to you, period. I don't want to talk to you now. I don't have anything to talk to you about. You and me, we've had it." She gave a little wave of her hand.

"Look, about last night . . ." He had almost forgotten about last night, the drinking and the woman called Lottie. He would have to think of something good to tell her.

"Frankly, I'm not interested." Essie sat down on the couch and crossed her legs, smoothing her skirt down over her knees. This made James Lee even more uncomfortable. Now he was the only one standing in the center of the living room. As large as the room was, he felt too big for it in his wrinkled clothes. He did not know this Essie. She was too calm. He wanted an argument or anything that would make her someone he recognized.

He said, "I only wanted to explain."

She returned, "You don't have to. You can go home now—or wherever it is you spend your nights."

He was being dismissed like a small boy who had come asking for something and had been refused. For a moment he felt it would be better to walk out of the apartment and try to forget the whole thing, but that would mean he had been defeated. He forced himself to laugh. Then he started shouting at her.

"Why, just look at little Essie. Where do you get off? You're nobody to me, you understand, and I mean *nobody!* I picked you up and I can drop you just like that. Where do you get off sitting up in this apartment putting on airs like a two-bit whore—"

She was stung. The viciousness hurt and shocked her out of her calm. She jumped to her feet.

"Nobody asked you to come up here," she yelled. "Why don't you just go away somewhere and leave me alone? I don't want nothing to do with you, and I mean *nothing!*"

Now that she had lost her temper, he felt he was on even ground. His voice mocked her. "If you're mad about last night why don't you say so? I come up here to explain something and you start acting like a fool—"

"You're the fool but you just don't know it," Essie said. "That's right. You don't know it and you never will know it, but you're the fool."

His words slipped out easily. "Here I've been thinking it was time we were getting married—"

"I wouldn't have you on a bet."

Their words clashed against each other. She was standing close to him, flinging her words into his face. He put his arm around her waist and snatched her to him. It seemed the natural thing to do.

Then everything went wrong. Something, perhaps a thousand such scenes in the movies, had made him expect that she would, after a moment's resistance, give herself to his embrace. But she twisted and she struggled, she kicked and she screamed, and he had to let her loose. Struggling for breath, she fell against the wall.

Then he knew he had to hit her. He had to punish her for what he was feeling. He had made a fool of himself, and she was the cause of it. But if he beat her, hurt her, she would know whether he was a man or not.

She must have known what he was thinking, for she stood quite still, almost in a crouch against the wall. But even as he raised his hand he knew that he was not going to strike her. This was not the way he had wanted it to be. It was all messed up. James Lee Cooley, he thought, what the hell are you up to now? You don't have the slightest idea. Just plain mixed up, that's what you are, Cooley. He lowered his hand and cursed —not Essie this time, not himself, but everything. He opened the door and walked out of the apartment.

Essie did not move for several moments. She continued to stare ahead of her as if he were still there. Then, suddenly, Essie thought she knew something that she had not known before, something that helped to explain everything that had happened. It surprised her because it was not about James Lee but about herself.

16

James Lee fought off all thinking as he wrenched the wheel of the car, jerking it out of its parking area and merging it into the southbound traffic of Riverside Drive. He had no destination, yet he drove with a fury, switching incautiously from one lane to the other, jumping traffic lights before they turned green. He rigorously avoided thinking about Essie. He felt as if he were being chased.

At One hundred and twenty-fifth Street he swung eastward under the elevated subway at Broadway. At Amsterdam Avenue a white man and woman with luggage gave him a frantic hail. Dammit, he thought, there's a three-dollar job to La Guardia or International Airport. But he passed them by because he did not want to stop the car. He sped on, catching the lights at St. Nicholas and Eighth Avenues.

He came to a sudden halt when he swung his car south on Seventh Avenue and plowed into the rear of a brand-new Cadillac that was double-parked in front of the Theresa Hotel. The noise from the crash barely made itself heard over the traffic sounds of the intersection, but those people standing nearby turned to look. Some of them pushed their way toward the scene of the accident. James Lee was unhurt, for he had braced himself when he saw he would not be able to stop his car in time. Sitting behind the wheel of the car with the people coming toward him, he took a deep breath, closed his eyes, and tried to relax.

There are a thousand stories about Negroes and Cadillac automobiles, of which probably nine hundred and ninety-five are not true. But the very prevalence of these stories testifies to the high regard that Negroes, like other underprivileged groups, hold for a Cadillac car. It is not just a better-than-average piece of machinery that takes you from one place to the other; it is a symbol of accomplishment, of triumph. When you drive a fishtail Cadillac you're serving notice that the world is no longer kicking you. The situation has been reversed, and you are kicking hell out of *it*, riding it like a bronco buster, breaking it in to fit your style. They say, "A Caddie is due respect," meaning not the car but the man who is driving it. They say, "Man, that woman ought to be riding in a Cadillac," meaning that she is good to look at, and, if they had their way, they would see that she had the best of everything. A woman who is not so favored has no business in a Cadillac. Many a young man whose fortune has taken a sudden turn for the better has traded in not only his Ford or his Chevrolet but also his woman.

This particular Cadillac was a powder-blue affair with immaculate white sidewall tires and bumpers trimmed in sparkling chromium. On the previous Saturday night the young owner had managed an extraordinary run of luck by throwing seventeen passes in a floating crap game. Each time he had left his winnings on the table and they had multiplied. On the seventeenth pass he broke the game. Sunday had been a day of acute frustration for him because all the car dealers were closed. But this very morning, he had gone to the showroom and bought his Cadillac for cash. When the collision came he was standing under the Theresa Hotel marquee talking with his cronies, some of whom had made generous contributions to the game on Saturday.

He turned and saw that it was his car, but he could not believe what he saw. He drew in his breath sharply and closed his eyes, then opened them again. It was true: there was really a yellow taxicab setting up on the rear end of his powder-blue Cadillac. He turned pale with rage, and from his head he snatched his hat, an expensive Panama straw (also new), slammed it to the sidewalk, and stamped on it with both feet. Clenching his fists, he looked up at the sky and swore a long and terrible oath that would have shocked and offended many of the bystanders had they all not felt as he did, that a man with a Cadillac had certain sacred and divine rights and that among these was immunity from collision.

Flanked by his companions, he walked weakly toward the scene of the accident. He attempted to regain some of the calm he had felt that morning. "Well, I'll be a monkey's uncle!" he said. "Boy, the good Lord just don't like colored folks." His friends tried to cheer him up. "Don't worry, man, you got to get paid. All those taxis are insured." He shook his head. "But, man, it'll never be like it was. Never."

Glumly James Lee and the unhappy Cadillac owner went through the formalities of exchanging credentials. While each was copying down information about the other, bystanders helped to untangle the automobiles. When the ceremony was over, James Lee drove away toward the garage.

"Jesus Christ Bloody Mary! Look at that!"

They were all watching as James Lee parked the car. The mechanics stared over the upstairs railing and Evaline came to the door to see what Danny was yelling about. Well, let them watch, thought James Lee as he prepared himself for what he knew would be an uncomfortable scene. Just so they don't start anything with me.

Danny tramped loudly down the metal steps and took a quick look at the car. "I'll be damned, a front end!" At all garages the driver was considered at fault if the front end of his car was damaged. Front ends ran up the insurance rates because they indicated the garage employed careless drivers.

"How did this happen, Cooley?"

"I ran into a guy."

"You mean it was your fault?" Even with a front end a New York hackie never admitted he was at fault. It was against tradition.

"Yeah, I guess that's what I mean," said James Lee. "I was at fault."

I don't have to stand here and be grilled by this punk, thought James Lee. He turned to Evaline and said, "Give me one of those accident forms, will you, Evaline?"

"Well, hell's bells!" Danny called. "Wait a minute, will you, and tell me what happened."

"I'll put it all down on the accident form and you can read it."

"I don't want to read it, I want to hear it—from you!"

"You gonna have to read it."

"Well, get a load of him, will you, fellas?" Danny spoke to his audience of mechanics, who were following every word from the second floor. "He brings in one of our cars half wrecked and he can't even take time to tell me about it."

He walked toward James Lee, who thought: He's just like that Marine poster in front of the Apollo Theater on One hundred and twenty-fifth Street, with his blond hair and blue eyes. He's the clean-cut American boy like the movie heroes, and I guess I'm scared because he's just as big as I am, but this is one day he can get a fight if he wants one.

Danny lowered his voice. "Look, sonny, I'm just the dispatcher around here, you know?"

"I don't care who you are—" James Lee was conscious of Evaline standing in the doorway— "and who the hell do you think you're calling sonny?"

"Look, Jackson, all I ask—"

"—and what's this Jackson business? My name's not Jackson. You know my—"

"—to hell with what your name is. I don't give a—"

James Lee swung first, a hard-aimed right that he did not know he was going to throw. But it was the next logical thing to do. Then all the accumulated fury and frustration exploded, and there were not just James Lee, Negro-American, and Danny O'Halloran, Irish-American, squaring off at each other in a taxi garage. James Lee was facing all the people who had irritated him all day, all the confusion that had kept him from understanding. There was Essie who was trying to show him up and make him feel small and inferior, and his father who was making a fool of himself, and McGowan with his crazy ideas, and the white man who had called him George and left a twenty-cent tip for the privilege. O'Halloran had none of this to drive him on, and he had been caught by surprise. He fought well because he had been in street fights and barroom tussles before, but there was nothing outside the natural desire to win and keep from getting hurt that impelled him.

James Lee thought, I will kill him if I can or I'll make him wish he was dead. When Danny caught him by the shoulders and slammed him to the floor he got up thinking, He's a good wrestler and I'll have to stay out of his reach. Swing now and keep him off, swing now and move right and move left and swing and keep on moving because if he catches hold of me I'm done for. But Danny did catch hold of James Lee's head with his left hand, pushing it down and slapping it with several cutting rights that left James Lee struggling for consciousness. In desperation he thought, I'll break his guts, and he brought his knee up into Danny's stomach and he heard the wind break from the Irishman's mouth. James Lee stepped back and with one vicious blow to the head he staggered Danny, who was dazed and fighting to catch his breath. With short, chopping blows James Lee beat against the dispatcher's head, thinking, Goddamit! get down, down, down. Finally O'Halloran was on one knee and then the other. A grunt of final effort tore from James Lee's lips as he slammed the heel of his right hand down on the back of Danny's neck. The dispatcher sprawled face downward with a deep groan, unconscious.

Neither Evaline nor the mechanics had moved, had hardly breathed, during the few savage moments of the brawl. Now for another full minute they stood as if impaled by what they had seen. Then the mechanics began running down the metal stairs, setting up a jarring racket. Evaline stared at the unconscious figure of Danny, stifling a scream with her hand over her mouth.

James Lee, breathing heavily, turned and stumbled toward the garage entrance. Come and get your blond god, he thought. He felt good. He had been afraid of this fight, but now he had won it, and he knew that this was the way life ought to be, full of gigantic struggles that were won in the end. He had no thought now of Danny or the police or of finding another job. He was full of himself and the problems that were closest to him. The edge was on him and he knew he could hack his way through those problems like a steel ax. On the street people noticed the bruises and the blood and made a path for him. He wanted to smile, but his lips were swollen. That's right, he thought, get out of my way. He plunged on through the crowded streets toward Harlem.

17

Hubert stood on the One-hundred-and-twenty-fifth-Street bridge that looks southward over Harlem toward downtown Manhattan. The bridge is of steel and concrete. On a hot day no one ever walks across because it intensifies the heat like an oven. There was the constant blare of automo-

bile horns and occasionally the groan of an old
boat as it chugged down the narrow Harlem river.
There were many other sounds: the drone of an
airplane dropping toward La Guardia Field, the
beat and grunt of a jukebox going full volume in
a bar down on Eighth Avenue, the sudden roar
of baseball fans in the Polo Grounds. Beneath all
these separate noises, pushing more persistently,
was the great hum of the city. It was like an or-
chestra with a thousand bass viols constantly re-
peating a single, groaning note. If you concentrated by deliberately shutting out the other
sounds, you could hear it, the drone of millions
of lives spending themselves in stifling intimacy.

Hubert grasped this humming with his attention, wrapped himself in it, and there he existed
for a while. He was absolutely alone now, and his
isolation was complete and different from any he
had ever experienced before. This was a complete
involvement with thought: He considered each of
his problems, reacted to a thousand irritations,
and wished for pleasures. It was passionate, it was
sensuous, and every inch of him was alive, hot,
and tingling. No one really mattered when he was
like this, neither Gertrude nor the boy nor what
they thought of him. It was almost painful, as
if his skin had been stripped away and the least
speck of dust caused a sensation. A thought could
make him cry or yell out in anger.

Already two of his numbers, the four and the

one, had played. It would soon be time for the third race. There was nothing unusual about his being only one digit away from a winner. He had come as close before without winning. Whenever this had happened, new enthusiasm had been born on the spot for the next day's number. Six days a week he had a chance to win, and this was what kept him going. When he had tentatively selected his number for the next day, he would turn it over in his mind, switching the digits to different positions. He would speak it aloud, accenting different syllables. He would rub his tongue over his lips, tasting the number as surely as if it were a tangible thing. Once a number had passed this inspection, nothing could shake him in his determination to play it.

But today Hubert knew that all of that was over, that he would never play another number again. He knew his time had come and that the last digit would be a seven. Hubert was talking to God about it. It was long overdue, his hitting the numbers, but God was, after all, a just God who made things come right in the end. God would have to help him a little further. There was the matter of Sister Clarisse. Nor did Hubert underestimate the difficulties of setting himself up in business in a new city. Once all of this had been taken care of, God could forget about him. Hubert would take care of himself.

The noises from the traffic jam on the bridge

pushed their way into Hubert's thoughts. He had been standing in the sun and he was drenched with perspiration. He walked toward the barbershop at the crest of the hill where One hundred and fifty-fifth Street joins St. Nicholas Avenue.

The fans in the shop droned. The barber was called Smitty. He was in his thirties, already fat, with the beautifully contoured lips of a man who enjoys talking whenever the opportunity presents itself. He and his customer were discussing a murder that had recently occupied the front pages of the Negro newspapers.

"The guy was crazy for playing around with a chick like that. Him with a wife and five kids." Smitty's scissors moved with a rhythmic chatter around the man's head. He had finished the haircut sometime before, but he would never let the customer know it until the conversation was finished or another customer entered. "She was bound to kill him if his wife didn't get him first. The cat never had a chance."

"She swore it was his gun and she took it away from him." Both men laughed.

Smitty nodded toward Hubert who entered just then. "Hiya, Mister Hubert, you're next."

"No, Smitty, I don't think I need one today." Hubert cleared his throat. "What was the last one?"

"A seven," said Smitty. "Can you beat that? I've been playing five-twenty-nine for a month now and can't come near it. A poor man ain't got no win."

"You said it," said the customer.

"Thanks, Smitty," said Hubert. He walked out of the shop.

"As I was saying," continued the customer, "some of the smart boys are laying odds that that little girl will never serve a day. Somebody told me—and this boy ought to know because he's got good connections himself—that that little girl has some of the right folks behind her from downtown."

"Well," said Smitty, summing it up, "it's a woman's world any way you look at it." A new customer had just walked in. "You're next," said Smitty, and with a flourish he finished the haircut.

Hubert was choked full with feeling, and the hot tears flowed easily. The hum of the city enveloped him in a new way, becoming for him a song of triumph.

As he walked toward John Lewis's apartment he saw again familiar objects of Harlem, the occasionally familiar face without a name. These people . . . his people . . . these Negroes . . . he was not angry with them any more, not resentful, not concerned with them. They could not hurt him any more. He was surprised to find that he really felt sorry for them, for all the Harlem black and brown and yellow folk, all the colored people all over the world who had never made it. Good-by, you poor fools, Hubert said to Harlem. God bless you. Soon Hubert would push them into the past like a bad dream.

John Lewis wore a large grin when he opened the door and looked down at Hubert.

"Man," he exclaimed, "am I sorry I ever laughed at you!" John Lewis gave a low whistle and slapped Hubert on the back. "You sure must've got up on the right side of the bed this morning, Mister Hubert. That's a lot of money you've got coming."

Hubert was uncomfortable. He did not like to be slapped on the back. He shifted his weight from one foot to the other.

"What are you going to do with all that money, Mister Hubert?" asked John Lewis.

"Oh, I've got a few ways to spend it," answered Hubert.

John Lewis said, "Well, I know this ain't no social call. You want to get your hands on that loot and I don't blame you."

"Well, I want it as soon as I can get it."

"I tell you what I'm going to do," John Lewis said. "Just because it's you, I'm going and pick it up myself. Suppose I bring it by your house at, say, seven o'clock, huh? How's that for speed?"

"That'll be fine," said Hubert.

On the way to the door John Lewis slapped Hubert on the back again. "Man, this is your lucky day, huh?"

"I'll see you at seven," said Hubert. It was not his lucky day. He was receiving his due. Life was settling its account with him. No luck about it.

As soon as the door closed behind Hubert, the smile vanished from John Lewis's face. He pushed his hand into his trousers' pocket and jerked out the money he had there. He crushed the bills in his big fist and hurled the green ball against the wall. It landed silently and bounced back to the couch. John Lewis sat down heavily and squeezed the ball again. "Well, kiss me one time!" he exclaimed. He gave himself a solid slap across the forehead. "Ada! Ada!" he called to his wife, who was napping in the bedroom. When he heard her mumble in her sleep he yelled, "Get up and come on out here!" He bit his lips, he cursed, he scratched his head and drove his fist into the couch. "Goddamn!" he growled as he lit a cigarette with unsteady hands. He unraveled the ball of money and walked over to the window, where he tore it into little green bits. He held a hand out the window, where a suggestion of a breeze caught up the green flakes and scattered them over the Harlem streets.

"John Lewis, boy," he said glumly, "you're a fool." For once in his life he was sure he knew what he was talking about.

18

Hubert looked at women again—not a particular one, but all of them—in a great sensuous conglomerate. He was the young male animal appraising each female he passed on the street. The young woman with the green outfit was easy to look at, and those earrings set her chestnut-brown complexion off just right. Hubert reflected that in all the world there was nobody who could beat a colored woman wearing earrings.

And it seemed to him that the women were taller than they used to be. At One hundred and twenty-fifth Street he paused to look at the young girl who stepped down from the bus. She was tapioca-colored, with red lips. Around her waist was a wide belt that matched the deep black leather bag she was carrying. Hubert wondered what in the world she would want with a bag so large. She had fine legs, slender yet strong. As she walked away, Hubert concentrated on the swing of her hips and the way her tight skirt emphasized the swing of her thighs.

She was taller than Hubert by two or three inches. He could not remember women being so tall when he was young and really after them. They had been good-looking, all right. Yes, indeed, women had always been pretty when a man was on top and had life where he wanted it, but Hubert did not think they had been so tall.

He walked on. Now he had more to do than watch young girls. There was a woman, a real flesh-and-blood woman waiting for him although she did not know he was coming.

Surprise and disapproval were on Sister Clarisse's face when she opened the door. She had not forgotten their conversation earlier that afternoon. "Mister Hubert!" she frowned. "Twice in one day? What will people think?"

Without waiting for an invitation he walked past her into the room. "It hit," he said.

"What did?" she asked.

"My number. It came just like I played it."

"Good for you," said Sister Clarisse, who was still wondering why he had returned to her apartment. "How much did you hit for?"

"Seven dollars," he announced.

"Aw, gowan," Sister Clarisse laughed. She knew that no one ever hit the numbers for seven dollars except big gamblers and people like that. With poor colored folks a hit for seven cents was more likely.

Hubert said, "That's more than four thousand dollars I got coming."

His seriousness frightened her. "Mister Hubert, you're joking, aren't you?"

"Not a bit," he answered, then added with a bold flourish, "not a damned bit."

The language was unusual for her apartment, but she took no notice of it. "Well, my goodness," she said weakly and sat down on the couch.

"This is what I was talking about when I was here a few hours ago, Sister Clarisse, only I just didn't know how soon it was coming. Here's our chance, yours and mine."

Sister Clarisse was only happy in a routine she understood. Problems bothered her because she did not know how to begin to handle them. She had never solved a major problem in her life. There had always been someone else to take care of them for her or she had left them to take care of themselves. Now she felt trapped. This man standing in front of her actually had ideas about the two of them going away together. It occurred to her that a woman with good intentions could get into a lot of trouble by just being nice to a man.

"I've been unhappy and dissatisfied for a long time, and you probably have, too. For more than ten years I've been waiting to kiss Harlem and New York good-by and go somewhere and start all over. All I needed was a little money to buy myself in because I found out a long time ago that a man has to own something to be on the inside. He needs money in the bank and a check book in his pocket. That's the only thing that makes him somebody."

Now, somehow, he was on the couch beside her and she had not even noticed that he was so near until he spoke again.

"I'm a man you could live with because I'm a man who could love you and be a partner with you in everything. We're not children any more— I'll be fifty-one my next birthday. I figure that we've got a little good living coming to us, Clarisse. Now, if you say yes, by eight o'clock tonight we'll be on our way to a new life together."

It was a wild idea. From time to time she had thought of doing wild and irresponsible things, but she had never been what she would call "bad." She raised her eyes and looked at Hubert. Yes, she liked his face. It was a man's face, smooth and strong. She liked the heavy black hair of his mustache, the firm lips. But the eyes bothered her. They seemed brown at first and yet darker, almost black. And intense, like the eyes of a troublesome boy. He had the eyes of a wild boy with wild dreams. Such dreams had to be beaten out with the practicality of adulthood. A man of fifty-one had no business with such eyes.

"Are you coming, Clarisse?"

Once, when she was seventeen and still a girl in Alabama, she had spent several months with relatives in another county. There had been a boy with such eyes, a restless boy, intense and passionate, who spoke to her of the wildest things. They had said that he drank and gambled and would never amount to anything, but none of that had mattered to her. She had given more of herself to him than to any man since. She had loved him. But nothing ever came of it. What happened? . . . a quarrel? She could not remember. And later, when she heard that he had been killed in an ugly gin-mill brawl, she cried for days. Later she came to realize that everybody had been right about him all along. Loving that boy was the last irresponsible act she had ever committed.

Hubert was waiting. She had to say something.

Then she saw them as they really were. She was forty-eight and a widow. No matter what some jealous folk said, she led a good, Christian life. Her husband had been a deacon of Little Calvary. Hubert was a man with a family, and everybody said he was peculiar in the head. Suppose she were to do the crazy thing he proposed? That would really give the sisters something to talk about. She could see them now, buzzing around Sister Gertrude with their sympathy and advice. No, Sister Clarisse would never give them any real ammunition to use against her. Besides, she was a good Christian woman and would never dream of doing such a thing.

She smiled and her laugh fluttered. "Well, Mister Hubert, my goodness! What would everybody say?" She knew it sounded childish and silly, but how else could she put it? You could not come right out and talk about a thing like that.

Hubert stood up. He looked at her for only a moment. Then he turned and walked out of the apartment. The vacant smile lingered on Sister Clarisse's face for several minutes. Her feeling of relief was tinged with sharp regret as she stared at the closed door, and she only remembered to remove the smile when she turned her eyes away.

19

At first the coming of the seven did not ring a bell with the corner bums at all. They lounged dispiritedly outside the Crystal Bar and went through a variation of their daily routine.

"Boy, money and me, we hate each other."

"You and me both, Pops."

"And here I am, dry as a nun's tit."

"Boys, I would put my last suit in hock and get us all a drink, but I did that yesterday."

"If my old lady would straighten up and act right, I could get a drink for us. But since she got this job of hers, she's acting kind of cool toward me."

"It wouldn't be so bad if I had come close to the damned number, but God knows that figure wasn't supposed to be no four-seventeen."

"I'm gonna quit playing myself. That's a promise."

"Yeah, no use making those number boys rich when the number is running wrong all the time."

Suddenly Flash gave himself a hard slap on the head and stamped his foot on the sidewalk. "Well, I'll be!" he yelled.

"What's ailing you, Flash?"

"Boys, don't none of us ever deserve another taste of sneaky pete." Flash snatched his hat from his head and slammed it against the wall. He gave the trash can a hard kick and sent it spinning into the street. "Man, ain't none of us got no sense at all."

"Well, get hold of yourself, man, and tell us what's happening."

"That's the number old man Hubert gave us this morning. Don't you remember? Four-seventeen. That's just what he said. I remember it because my aunt lives at Four-seventeen St. Nicholas Avenue, and at the time I said to myself, I ought to play that number just in case. Ooooooh!"

He moaned and groaned and slapped himself on the cheeks with the palm of his hands. He finally lay down on the sidewalk with arms outstretched, pleading, "Somebody please kill me dead right this minute. Anybody as stupid as me don't deserve to live."

This behavior was not unusual for a numbers player who thinks his own foolishness has caused him not to hit. But there was no one to comply with Flash's request because all his companions now recalled the number Hubert had given them and each of them went through the same kind of antic. It now developed that each had thought the number was good but for one reason or another had not played it. Each confessed that his own stupidity had lost him a fortune.

After a while they began to speculate on how much money Hubert had won.

"Well, you know what John Lewis said: that Hubert don't never bet less than five dollars."

"Great day in the morning! Count that up, Flash. You're good at figures."

Flash calculated and told them the total. They all agreed that it was a magnificent sum, and then the discussion naturally turned to what they would do if they had that much money. The consensus was that a down payment on a Cadillac would be worth while and the rest would go toward parties, women, and good wine and whisky.

192

When James Lee approached, one of them yelled, "Jesus, look at the kid."

"He looks like a truck backed over him."

"Two trucks."

The blood from James Lee's nose had dried into a black stain on his shirt. His jaw was puffed and one of his eyes was swollen.

"Boy, look at your hair standing at attention."

"And your eyes going in every which direction."

"And your jaw trying to take off like the mumps."

"Your old man's done hit the jackpot, boy."

"What are you guys talking about?"

"Don't you know about four-seventeen?"

He did not know. They told him. He hurried on.

Earlier, when Gertrude had returned home, she had sat in the big overstuffed chair and begun to cry for the first time in many years. No, life had not been good to her, but she had taken everything without a whimper. She had known that life was something you did something about, you *acted*, so there had never been any need for tears. But now there was nothing to do. She felt herself a raw, tender thing who had been roughly handled and hurt. At first she had cried softly. But these tears seemed to open up a well within her, and her large body shook with great sobs.

She choked and coughed and cried until she was exhausted. After this she felt relieved. She closed her eyes and went to sleep. She did not hear James Lee when he came in. He went to the bathroom where he washed and changed his clothes.

"Mama."

She opened her eyes. James Lee was kneeling beside her. Although he had washed, she could see the bruises.

"Honey, what in the world happened to you?"

"What happened to you? You've been crying."

"No. I was just sleeping," she said.

"Where's Pop?"

"Lord, I don't know. He took our last seven dollars out of here this morning and I ain't seen him since."

"Did he say what number he was going to play?"

She said, "No, I don't think so."

James Lee asked, "Did he say anything about four-seventeen?"

Gertrude sat up now, fully awake. "I remember he said he had a dream last night and he was going to play four something or other."

"It was four-seventeen," James Lee said. "He told the guys on the corner. If he played it he hit it."

"Call John Lewis and be sure."

James Lee went to the phone and found an old booklet with the pages curled at the edges.

He thumbed through it, found a number, and dialed it.

"Hello, Ada. This is James Lee. Do me a favor and ask John Lewis if Pop was right today." He listened a moment, then said, "Thanks." He hung up the receiver.

"Pop hit for seven dollars," said James Lee. "John Lewis is supposed to bring the money by here in a little while."

Gertrude said nothing. He asked, "What're you going to do, Mama?"

She sighed. "I don't see nothing I can do. I guess if a man hits for that much money we ought to be happy."

The front door opened and Hubert came in.

Without speaking, he went to the hall closet and took out his bag, the one he had never used before, the one that for three years had been setting in the closet with new clothes in it. He went into the kitchen and came back with a cloth that he used to wipe away the dust. After unfastening the two straps, he unsnapped the lock and laid the bag open on the couch. James Lee watched, somehow fascinated by his father's slow, deliberate movements. Each activity was logical, growing out of one thing and leading to another. But all together they made no sense.

Hubert came out of the bathroom with his toilet articles. He carefully wrapped them in newspaper and placed them in a compartment of the bag. James Lee's voice sounded weary as he spoke.

"Pop, what do you think you're doing?"

"I'm packing a bag, boy," said Hubert, "as any fool can plainly see." He went to the closet and took out a suit.

"You going someplace?"

"That's right," said Hubert. "You get the idea."

"You mean you're leaving home—Mama and everything?"

"That's right."

James Lee was suddenly exasperated. "You're crazy, you know that! Just plain crazy. Why, you little jerk! You couldn't make it on your own with fifty thousand dollars if you didn't have somebody to play nursemaid to you." He yelled, "You're a number one first-class jerk!"

The words had no effect on Hubert, who went into the bedroom. James Lee turned to Gertrude. "Mama, aren't you going to say something? Try to stop him?"

"Not a word. Let him go. I can't take it any more." Her voice was low and tense and she was trying to keep from yelling.

When Hubert came back to the room James Lee said, "If you're trying to hurt Mama, you can forget it. You've already done that."

"Not trying to hurt nobody," he said. "I'm just leaving. Never did like it around here. I've been wanting to get away for many a long year." He went on with his packing.

James Lee looked at Gertrude, really looked at her, and saw a large, ungainly woman, tired and beaten. He remembered old snapshots he had seen in an album that used to be around the house. They were photographs of Gertrude and Hubert when they were young. James Lee used always to wonder why his mother had married his father. She was very handsome. James Lee always remembered his mother's dark, beautiful eyes in the photographs. They had been large and eager, and he had wondered that his mother was ever so young. Now—he forced himself to think it—she was almost ugly, so large, so worn.

"Goddamn you!" He spat the words at his father. James Lee had never cursed Hubert before nor had his mother ever heard him use such language. He rushed out of the apartment.

Hubert and Gertrude heard him walk quickly through the hallway and down the steps outside. Then, for a while, in this room where man and wife were, there was silence. Finally Hubert brought more clothes from the closet and went on with his packing.

Again James Lee walked the streets without seeing. The sun seemed beyond the Hudson now, and the heat was lifting. As the coming-home rush hour approached, activity increased on Lenox Avenue. At One hundred and twenty-fifth Street the subway seemed to cough up people who pushed their way through the exits and dispersed. James Lee felt the rumble of the heavy old Seventh Avenue trains below the street as they dragged themselves farther uptown. A girl in a blue bonnet, somehow pretty without rouge or lipstick, stood near one exit selling religious magazines. Shoeshine boys in tight-legged motorcycle dungarees stood near the corner and yelled at prospective customers. People paused in front of the newsstand to snatch a *News* or *Mirror* or a *Jet* magazine that they began to read while waiting for the traffic light to change. A bus already packed with passengers roared past its stop and halted in the middle of the block to discharge some of its occupants. Some of the people who had been waiting at the stop set up a yell of protest and pushed down the street toward the bus. A mounted policeman, a black man with dark glasses, galloped down the block and drove the people back onto the curb. The smell of grilled frankfurters came from a nearby stand where a dark-brown girl was irritably reminding the crowd that she only had two hands. The soft, steady daytime beat of Lenox Avenue shifted. Picking up its darktime rhythm, it became feverish, mad, syncopated.

James Lee turned west on One hundred and twenty-fifth Street. He was biting his lip and talking to himself. He wished he could have said to his father and mother what was on his mind

and in his heart. Once they had loved each other.
. . . But people did not think like that, did they
. . . about love? Not really. *But they had loved
each other.* What else could you call it? And
something had caused that love to break down
over the years. You had to have something else
besides love to keep from turning out like his
parents. You had to become better or you became
worse. It was as simple as that. His father had
been an okay person, but look at him now . . . a
mean, ugly little man who was hurting the only
one who cared anything about him. His mother
. . . those eyes in the old snapshots . . . Why,
my God! They reminded him of Essie!

He stopped abruptly in the middle of the sidewalk. The people pushed past him.

Twenty-five years ago his mother had been
about the same age as Essie. She had met this
fellow named Hubert and decided that this was
the man with whom she would spend her whole
life. Look what a mess they had made of it.
Could the same thing have happened to him and
Essie? James Lee Cooley had given her a rough
time just like Hubert Cooley's son might be expected to.

He began walking again. His steps quickened.
He turned at St. Nicholas and headed uptown.

Where did I get these silly ideas that I've been
carrying around with me, he was thinking. Treat
the girls rough, they like it . . . variety, man,

the spice of life . . . screw 'em all while you can . . . do her wrong before she does you wrong. How many times have I wanted to really talk to Essie?

McGowan had said it! Life is a precious thing and you don't fill it up with dumb ideas just because there are plenty of them around. Now I see. There are all kinds of things trying to pull a man down, but mostly it's his own ideas. You've got to stay on your toes and you've got to keep thinking for yourself . . . always thinking for yourself . . . it's your only hope.

Suddenly James Lee was conscious of his direction. He broke into a run toward Iretha's apartment, where Essie was.

20

The afternoon rush hour in Grand Central Station is a long one that begins at about half-past three and only subsides toward seven o'clock. In the vacant white lights that spill down from the high chandeliers thousands of people rush toward New York Central commuter trains that carry them out of the city's heat to small green residential towns farther north. During these hours the station is like a well-organized but over-crowded beehive. From the world's busiest center, Manhattan's midtown, the car horns, the millions of voices, the thousand other distinct sounds, combine into a single persistent din that envelops the station and seeps through its walls. The hollow voices of the public address system and the clatter of racing footsteps echo off the high hard ceiling.

The young Negro woman who walked down into the station from the west-side entrance carried her head high. She had been shopping, and, besides her overnight bag, she carried a large hat box filled with her purchases. She moved with a jaunty step that was not without youthful grace. There were pride and sophistication in her walk, and anyone watching her would have said definitely that she knew where she was going and what she was going to do when she got there.

When you go through life being afraid, she was thinking, you're really asking for trouble. And you don't have to wait long before you get it. Poor little Essie. I just had to have a big strong man to lean on. I couldn't stand the thought of being alone in this big old city. He never took anything away from me. The things that counted, I gave. But I'm somebody too.

She stopped in front of the ticket window and bought a round-trip fare.

No wonder he wanted to hit me. If your pet dog starts acting up, you give it a beating. Well,

Essie, you live and learn. After I tell old lady Ornstein I quit, I'm coming back down here and live in this old town. That was all a lot of nonsense anyway, going up there. Just a case of being scared again. I'll get a job, go to night school . . . heck, I can even live with Iretha. Nobody scares me, not any more.

A frantic-looking young Negro man rushed into the west-side entrance and moved his eyes searchingly over the bustling crowd below. When he had found the person he was looking for he called out, but his voice was drowned in the great murmur of the station. He bounded down the marble staircase three at a time, jostling commuters and excusing himself as he rushed by them.

"Essie. Hey, Essie!"

He was so happy he had found her that he had forgotten how angry with him she must be. "Hey, Essie, it's me. Iretha told me what train you'd catch."

"Hi," she said as she returned his smile, but she kept on walking. For a moment he stood watching after her. Then he caught up and fell in step beside her.

"Hey, where're you going?"

"I'm going to White Plains." She did not slacken her pace nor did she look at him. He caught her by the elbow and gently pulled her to a halt.

"Hey, this is me. Remember James Lee? You know me."

"Yes, I remember you." She smiled. "I'll always remember you. Now I don't want to miss my train. Good-by, James Lee."

She walked through the gates that led to the tracks. He followed her onto the platform. He had to talk to her. He had to explain what he had been thinking and feeling. He caught up to her again.

"Look, Essie, about last night and that crazy stuff today in Iretha's apartment—" That wasn't the way he wanted to begin. "—Well, look, all that is dead and I know it now for what it was. I wish I could make you understand how different I feel. I've been looking at Mom and Pop and I know how a person can get mixed up the way I was. But listen to me, I don't want to be that way. I don't, Essie. Believe me."

She felt his sincerity. "James Lee, you and me, we've had all we can get from each other. I don't love you, not any more, and I don't think you ever gave a rap for me. Understand, I'm not blaming you. I thank you for what I got, the good times, the hard times, all of that . . ."

She paused. For the first time since she had known him he was listening to everything she was saying. Even this made her angry, and she knew she did not have to be, so long as she knew what she was going to do. But as she looked at him she could not keep her anger down.

"You pushed me around—" She stopped. She had not meant to shout. She spoke in a fierce whisper. "Well, nobody's pushing me around any more. That's all I'm trying to say."

She started to walk again, and he was beside her. She was crying now because she was thinking how wonderful everything could have been and how nasty and stupid it had turned out. She thought about the baby. She knew there were tears in her eyes, but she would not wipe them away. She said, "I'm crying because it didn't work out."

James Lee had been listening in silence. Glancing around, he saw something that made him stop so suddenly that she stopped too.

"What is it?" Essie asked.

"Baby, please don't get on the train yet," he said. "We've got to talk."

James Lee walked a few feet away into the path of a man who had just bought a ticket and, with overnight bag, was rushing to catch an express train that was taking on passengers on the other side of the platform.

> *He who fights and runs away*
> *Will live to fight another day*

was the crazy rhyme that repeated itself in John Lewis's mind. Some people had the luck and some people didn't. He had been going along just fine, with a great future, and then a crazy, stupid number like this 417 had to show up. Why hadn't he bet the money with the big bank in the first place instead of taking a silly chance? Four . . . one . . . seven . . . those three numbers could ruin a man's whole life. Together, the hits against him came to seven thousand dollars, and he did not have nearly that much. And his reputation! This was what really mattered. Well, no one could say he hadn't tried. He really wanted to pay off the winners. He and Ada had been on the phone two hours trying to round up some cash. They had called every big wheel they knew without any luck at all. Guys he had drunk with and gambled with, guys who could have raised the money with a telephone call—they had turned him down. When a new bank got busted, everybody swore it off. If his had been an old, established bank that suddenly came up two hundred thousand short—well, that would have been different. But those low-down rats would not back him for four thousand. They were willing to let him go under. But John Lewis was a big man and he would show them. This was what they called a temporary setback. A couple of months and he would be back. Numbers players are funny people. Right after they hit and don't get their money, they're liable to kill you. But give them a little time to think it over and they will chalk it up to experience. If that little guy, Mister Hubert, had been the only winner, there would be no need to leave town. But two of the others were the kind of low-class Negroes who were mean enough to start cutting and shooting. So the best thing for John Lewis was to absent himself until the storm blew over. Anyway, it might be a nice vacation for him and Ada up there in Syracuse in her mother's house. Ada would take care of the apartment and drive the car up later. Oh, yes, it was just a vacation because he would be back. New York was a big city and God knew that John Lewis was a big—

"Say, John Lewis. Where're you going?"

John Lewis stopped. James Lee was the last person in the world he expected to see. "Hey, man," laughed John Lewis. He put his big hand in James Lee's and tried to sound pleasant. "What are you doing down here?"

"Are you making a trip?" James Lee asked.

"Well, kind of . . ." John's mind was working frantically. "Say, did you know your old man just finished cleaning me out? Got to go dig up some more loot."

James Lee was puzzled. "You mean you already paid Pop?"

"Yeah," said John Lewis. "I got it a little quicker than I thought, so I took it on over. He's a rich man now." John Lewis's eyes shifted uneasily. He was trying to keep them looking directly at James Lee, but they moved away involuntarily.

"Say, what do you mean, he cleaned *you* out? I didn't know you had a bank of your own now. I thought you were still just writing them."

"Did I say *me?* What I meant was *us.* He cleaned us out." He was trying too hard to explain. He realized this as soon as James Lee did. "Well, man, there goes my train."

James Lee said, "Say, wait a minute. You're not trying to run out with my old man's money, are you?"

"All aboard," called the platform conductor.

John Lewis said, "Man, you must be crazy. I told you I've got to catch a train."

James Lee did not know what he was trying to do, but he felt he had to hold on to John Lewis. He reached out and caught him by the sleeve.

"What's the matter with you, boy?" yelled John Lewis. "You know better than to be pulling on my clothes. Have you lost your mind?"

"I think you're taking a powder. Look, John Lewis, my old man is counting on that money. It's like a sickness. He's got to have it so he can find out—"

"I don't know what you're talking about," John Lewis said. "I told you I already paid your old man." He pushed James Lee's arm away. Some of the passengers, seeing two heavyweight Negroes arguing, stepped off the train onto the platform hoping to see a fight.

"All aboard!" called the platform conductor with finality. The train creaked to a slow start.

"Look," said James Lee as he caught John Lewis's arm again, "stay and catch the next train—"

"Boy, I told you."

In one movement John Lewis jerked his arm free and dropped his bag near his feet. He was an ex-boxer with a quick job to do. Already James Lee was swinging a hard right that he blocked easily at the same time he hooked his own right into James Lee's stomach. John Lewis followed this up with a quick left to the jaw and a jarring right to the head. James Lee gasped. He fell face downward and lay there. John Lewis scooped up his bag and dashed for the moving train. He had only a few feet of platform left when he jumped onto the observation car. The train jerked into the tunnel and disappeared.

An elderly white man, one of those who had missed his train to see the fight, cautiously approached James Lee. "Are you all right?"

James Lee tried to clear his head and pushed himself to his knees. The jaw that Danny had bruised first now felt as if it no longer belonged to him.

"Are you all right?" The white man had sandy

hair and was carrying a battered briefcase. James Lee thought the man was grinning, but he could not be sure because his eyes were not focusing well. He felt hot and embarrassed. He tried to picture what all these white people were thinking of two Negroes fighting in Grand Central Station. It would give them something to talk about when they got home that night.

"I'm okay," he said. He wanted to yell at all the staring faces, but all the fight was out of him now. He felt Essie's hands helping him to his feet.

"You all right?" she asked.

"I guess so."

"What in the world was all that about?"

He told her briefly about John Lewis and his father. Then he asked, "Are we really through, Essie? I came down to ask you to try again."

"I'd like to try again," said Essie, "but you see, there's nothing left to try. No use trying to breathe life into what's dead. And it is dead . . . like our baby."

They were silent.

"All aboard." The platform conductor had walked across to the second train now.

"Good-by," she said.

"Good-by, Essie."

She touched his hand. Then she walked into the train. He watched her go, feeling strangely happy for her, although he felt cold and empty already. After a moment the train began to move.

One by one its cars were pulled into the tunnel. Essie was gone.

Evening approached Harlem. Hubert had taken his suitcase and set it on the small landing outside the vestibule. From there he would be able to see when John Lewis turned into One hundred and twenty-sixth Street from Lenox Avenue. He sat down on the suitcase to wait.

The news of the big hit had spread up and down the block. Many of the Cooley neighbors rushed through their dinners so they could see John Lewis when he brought the money. Coming home from work some of them had stopped to inquire, "You taking a trip, Mister Hubert?"

"Yep."

And when they had asked him where he was going he had smiled and said, "Any place that comes to mind."

When there was no one asking him questions, Hubert talked to himself. "A man hopes and prays all his life for something like this to happen, and when it comes he can't back down. It's a deal he makes with himself and that kind he can't break."

In their homes from time to time the children of the block had overheard their parents say that Hubert was crazy. Some of them now gathered under a street lamp a few yards away from the Cooley apartment. They played halfheartedly at their games. They were really watching Hubert and waiting for John Lewis. Hubert looked at them for a long time. Then he spoke aloud, softly, insistently.

"It's no good around here," he said. "You never get a chance to do any living. Babies are born here and old folks die here, but in between there ain't no living."

And later he said, "I don't blame Gertrude and I don't blame the boy. I tried to give both of them ambition and I found out that you can't do that. They never understood me. I don't believe I was born to spend my whole life on this street or any other street in Harlem. I've wanted to be too many grand and wonderful things to find out in the end that this was all I was ever meant to be."

It was almost completely dark when James Lee came down the street. Hubert did not seem to know him. The young man spoke gently, in a tired voice.

"No use waiting, Pop. John Lewis won't be here." James Lee explained what had happened at Grand Central, but when he finished he knew that Hubert had not listened to him. His father sat with his eyes fixed on Lenox Avenue.

James Lee said, "It's past eight o'clock, Pop. Believe me, he's not coming." He put his hand on Hubert's shoulder. "He never comes, Pop. Don't you see that? John Lewis never really comes."

Hubert did not answer. James Lee became conscious of people watching from nearby houses. He looked at the kids who had stopped their game under the streetlamp and were staring. James Lee went into the house. He would bring the old man in later. Now he wanted to tell his mother.

After a while Hubert gave a low chuckle of satisfaction. "They laughed at me and said I would never make it, but I did. Maybe it ain't true that every dog will have his day, but I'm going to have mine." He laughed and wiped the sweat from his forehead with the back of his hand.

Now he was tired. He felt as if he had no strength in any part of his body. He took a deep breath. "Come on, John Lewis, come on. I gave this street too much precious time. Gave it my youth, gave it my strength. Ain't gonna give it no more. Come on, John Lewis, come on."

A fire engine, clanging and hooting, roared down Lenox Avenue. Night settled over Harlem but brought no rest. The murmur of living, like the river, flowed on into the evening toward the dawn.